DOUBLE CROSS!

Slocum slipped the Colt Navy from its holster and waited. He knew this wasn't going to be an easy fight. Killing Gentry was too easy; they had to at least get the gold dust back from him.

"Gentry, look out!"

It took Slocum a split second to realize that Abrams had betrayed him. Counting on the guard being confused at the warning, Slocum spun and swung blindly. The barrel of his six-shooter hit the burly man on the temple. Gentry stumbled backward, and Slocum stepped out and cocked the pistol.

"I just wanted to say good-bye before I blew your thieving head off."

JAKE LOGAN

SLOCUM AND THE IDAHO BREAKOUT

BERKLEY BOOKS, NEW YORK

SLOCUM AND THE IDAHO BREAKOUT

A Berkley Book/published by arrangement with
the author

PRINTING HISTORY
Berkley edition/September 1989

ISBN: 0-425-11748-0

A BERKLEY BOOK ® TM 757,375
Berkley Books are published by The Berkley Publishing Group
200 Madison Avenue, New York, N.Y. 10016.
The name "BERKLEY" and the "B" logo
are trademarks belonging to Berkley Publishing Corporation.

PRINTED IN THE UNITED STATES OF AMERICA.

10 9 8 7 6 5 4 3 2 1

1

John Slocum tucked his battered canvas poncho more securely around his knees as he rode into the teeth of a late autumn storm. The cold wind cut at his face like a razor and threatened to rip away his Stetson. The scent on the wind worried him more than the physical discomfort. The wet smell made him wary of a full-blown winter storm coming off Idaho's Lost Mountain Range and its snow-capped, towering giant, Mount Borah.

"We're getting there," he said, patting his horse's neck. The animal turned and looked back at him, venom in the normally placid brown eyes. As much as he tried, the poncho wouldn't shield the horse from the savage wind. Even with his duster on under the poncho and every piece of clothing he had on under that, he shivered with every new gust. He knew what it must be like for the gelding.

Slocum snorted, and long silvery plumes of hot breath shot into the air, only to be ripped away by the wind. If he didn't get to Idaho City soon, he'd be a gelding too, his balls frozen off along the trail.

Not for the first time, he cursed himself for riding north from Salt Lake City. It had been warmer there, these vicious hints of a long, cold winter held at bay for another month into 1877 by the Wasatch Range. He reached under the poncho and touched the telegram folded twice and stuffed into his shirt pocket. The simple slip of yellow paper had brought him north. Too damned far north for his taste. If he couldn't get the business with Jesse Keegan squared away soon, he'd hightail it for warmer southern climes. Arizona appealed to him more and more as the storm blew around him.

The wind gasped even louder, sounding like a hard-rock miner with consumption. A particularly strong blast caused his horse to stumble. Slocum cursed a blue streak, but the words were rammed back down his throat by the increasingly frigid storm. He looked around for a place to hole up and ride out the tempest. The terrain didn't look promising. He was riding down into the valley holding Idaho City. Nearby caves might already be staked out by hibernating bears. Tangling with a half-asleep grizzly was the last thing in the world Slocum wanted to do right now. His fingers were so close to being frozen he couldn't even wrap them around the butt of his ebony-handled Colt Navy riding under his duster in its cross-draw holster.

"Damn you, Jesse Keegan," he said, deciding to keep riding and hope he reached shelter soon. "You're going to owe me for this one. I swear it!"

He and Keegan had been partners for over a year down in Utah Territory. The takings had been good but not good enough to keep Keegan from wandering on when he heard of gold strikes in Idaho's Lost Mountain Range. Wanderlust and Silas Abrams' constant yammering about the easy pickings to the north had decided Keegan to move on and leave Slocum behind. For Slocum's part, that was fine. He liked Keegan and trusted him as a friend—but he had no confidence in Abrams. The man's liquid silver tongue hid a soul of tarnished base metal.

Slocum had seen the man's kind before and didn't much cotton to them. All talk and no do. And Slocum didn't doubt that when Keegan needed a friend, he wouldn't find one in Silas Abrams. The man would always seek fair skies and the easy way out rather than doing what was right.

His horse stumbled again on an icy patch. Slocum dismounted and walked the horse. Being afoot didn't suit him any, but the slight refuge from the wind afforded by the horse's body let him experience a warmth he had forgotten hours back.

He came to the outskirts of Idaho City before he knew it. He wiped the water from his eyes; snow had begun blowing and had threatened to freeze his eyelids shut. In another month, he would never be able to survive wearing these clothes. He needed a more complete winter outfit before starting back to Salt Lake City.

It took him twenty minutes to find the town livery. A bored old man looked more interested in chewing on a piece of straw than in taking care of Slocum's horse. A silver dollar brought a spark of interest to his tired eyes, but not enough to suit Slocum.

"I don't want him neglected," Slocum warned. "He's a fine horse and deserves to be curried and fed."

"Don't go frettin' none about that, son," said the old man, pushing up the sleeves of his union suit. He wore a red-and-black checkered wool shirt open to the waist. Slocum wondered if he didn't feel any of the chill shaping up to winter, even inside the barn. It didn't look as if the old man did.

"I'll be back to see how the animal's faring," he said, meaning it. He had bought the gelding for fifty dollars from a horse trader in Utah and had been pleased as punch with the deal. The trader had sold cheap because he thought the gelding was pulling up lame. A bottle of Doctor Goble's Miracle Linment and some decent care had produced one fine and dependable mount. Slocum wasn't going to lose the horse to Idaho's first storm of the season.

"Do that. You might do yourself a favor and get something warm into your belly. My wife puts up a fine meal. If 'n you need a place to stay, we run a boardinghouse, too. A dollar a night and breakfast fit for a king." The old man tipped his head to one side and squinted at Slocum, as if judging him by the size of his bankroll. Whatever decision he came to seemed to find in Slocum's favor.

"Might take you up on that. I have to spend at least the night, then I'll probably be moving on."

"One night or a week. Don't make no never-mind to us. Martha enjoys cooking—and she's real good at it."

Slocum nodded and left, giving his horse one parting glance. The animal had settled down and was rolling about in the clean straw on the stall floor.

The storm caught the edge of his poncho and tugged mightily as he stepped back onto the street. He pulled the brim of his Stetson down to protect his eyes and made his way across the half-frozen street to the Mother Lode Saloon. He slipped through the door and yanked it shut behind him.

He had entered a new and wonderfully warm world. The smell of stale beer made his nostrils flare, and the sight of food on the bar made his mouth water.

A piano player made a poor effort to play without hitting flat notes, and four men sat at a table playing cards. Other than them and the barkeep, the Mother Lode looked mined out.

"Have a beer, mister?" asked the bartender.

"The pig's knuckles and pretzels free if I do?" asked Slocum.

"Go on, help yourself. It looks as if you could use

something stronger. That storm's been brewing for three days now. Don't usually see them come from Canada this time of the year. You get caught by surprise in it?"

"Surely did," Slocum allowed. He pointed to a bottle of Kentucky bourbon, even though he knew its heritage was far more likely to be the saloon's back room. He knocked back a quick shot, then tapped the side of the shot glass for another. The barkeep was only to happy to oblige.

"Yes, sir, it does get cold out on the trail," the man said, his watery eyes gleaming. Slocum looked to be the best customer he was going to have all day.

Slocum started to ask after Jesse Keegan when the door opened and a fresh blast of freezing air gusted through the saloon. He pulled his poncho up and moved his hand toward his Colt Navy. The man who had entered sported a battered star on his heavy coat.

"Afternoon, Sheriff," called the barkeep. Slocum turned so that he faced away from the lawman. Too many warrants were drifting around for his arrest. Some were legitimate, some weren't. Slocum didn't want to find out if this sheriff had a good memory for smeary pictures on old wanted posters.

"A terrible day outside, Josh, and it's gettin' worse by the minute. I swear, I never remember seein' a storm come this early and this hard in more'n fifteen years of prowlin' along the Snake and the Columbia."

The lawman cast a quick look in Slocum's direction, then turned to the whiskey the barkeep had put in front of him. Slocum was just beginning to relax when two more lawmen came in. The three men, all sheriffs from different parts of the territory, got to talking. They left the bar and went to a table in the back of the Mother Lode.

"Why so many lawmen?" Slocum asked the barkeep. The man poured him another drink and reluctantly took the folded scrip laid on the bar to pay for his binge. "Looks like there are enough to keep the whole damn territory clean of outlaws for a year."

"There's one or two more around besides them," said Josh. He scratched himself and stared at the sheriffs at the back of the saloon. "You must have come up from the south."

Slocum admitted that he had.

"There's been a raft of unease around here lately. Chief Joseph and his Nez Percé are kicking up a real fuss. Can't keep 'em down. Damned redskins are pillaging and making life miserable."

"That looks to be cavalry business, not a sheriff's concern."

"There's been other unpleasantness," the barkeep said. He drew out the word "unpleasantness" as if it burned his tongue saying it. "Gold mining is increasing again. There are more mines—good ones—starting up than at any time since the War."

Slocum nodded. The flood of gold from Idaho had drawn Jesse Keegan. A few quick hijacked gold shipments would put him on easy street, he'd said. Slocum knew that was Silas Abrams' opinion, not Keegan's, but the man had gone along with it. He started to ask after Keegan when the barkeep continued.

"Sheriff Morgan, yonder, he's a good man. He brought a prisoner in to the Territorial Prison just yesterday. A man name of Keegan had been giving everyone fits. Morgan ran him down and drug the son of a bitch back."

"What did Keegan do?"

Josh shrugged. "The usual. Robbed here and there. He and two accomplices knocked off a big gold shipment from Coeur d'Alene. That put everyone after 'em. Sheriff Mor-

gan tracked him down, caught him, and got him convicted."

"And?" Slocum guessed there was more.

"The slippery son of a bitch escaped. Took Morgan well
nigh a week to get him again. This time Keegan's locked
up secure behind the penitentiary walls. No man's going to
escape there, short of death or finishing his sentence."

"A hard prison?"

"The toughest north of Yuma," Josh said with some
pride.

Slocum wished he could share such civic pride in the
Idaho Territorial Prison. If Jesse Keegan was locked up
there, Slocum didn't think there was much chance of busting him loose.

He frowned. "How long ago did you say Keegan got
away?"

"About a week," said the barkeep. "Why?"

Slocum shook his head as if it were nothing. The timing
was all wrong. He couldn't imagine Keegan sending the
wire to him in Salt Lake City if he were running for his
life. Even more troublesome was the notion that Keegan
would ask him up and not mention any trouble. If Slocum
hadn't been lucky, he would have started asking around
and got himself noticed by the law. He might be doing time
in the pen alongside his friend.

"Thanks for the food and drink," Slocum said. He
downed the last of the whiskey, appreciating the warmth it
brought to his belly. It would last him through the night—
and into the next day, when he would start back for Salt
Lake City. Jesse Keegan was a friend and he owed him for
too many things to count, but he wasn't going to waste
time trying to get the man out of the Territorial Prison.
Even without the bartender's smug assurance about the
prison's invulnerability, Slocum had heard tales. The

prison was new, it was well guarded, and worst of all, winter was setting in.

That combination made rescuing Jesse Keegan impossible.

Slocum turned and started for the door when it opened, letting in a new flood of frigid air. The wind gusted past him, pinning his poncho against his body for a few seconds. The frost-covered man who had entered the Mother Lode Saloon forced the door shut against the wind and faced Slocum.

Slocum let out a soft sigh.

"Hello, Abrams," he said. "I was hoping I could get out of Idaho City without seeing you."

"Slocum," Silas Abrams said, ignoring everything the other had said. "I was sure you'd come."

"You sent the telegram, didn't you?"

"Jesse is in no position to." Abrams looked past Slocum at the table where the lawmen sat drinking and swapping lies. "Let's go where we can talk this over, private-like."

"We can talk about it here," Slocum said. The small man's furtive movements, his darting eyes, and the set to his body told him there was more to this than he wanted to know.

"Jesse's in a spot of trouble," Abrams started.

"He's in the damned Territorial Prison!"

"You heard. I sent the telegram so's we could get together and bust him out. We don't have much time. I hear Jesse's kinda busted up. The damned sheriff did it to him."

Slocum motioned to a table at the far side of the saloon from the lawmen. Something in the way Abrams spoke told Slocum the man was lying through his teeth. Abrams' refusal to lock eyes told Slocum even more. The man had not only started out lying, he kept at it.

What was he keeping back?

"You owe Jesse. You owe him more than this little favor. He saved your life down in Utah more times than you can count. He told me about it."

Slocum couldn't imagine Silas Abrams being the kind of man to stick by a friend who had the run of bad luck Keegan seemed to have. Abrams still hadn't looked him squarely in the eye.

"The bartender," said Slocum, "told me about Sheriff Morgan and the way he hunted Keegan down."

"It's true! He hunted him like an animal!"

"All for a simple robbery? Gold is precious, but not that damned precious."

"There was a guard or two shot up during the robbery," Abrams admitted. From his tone Slocum guessed who had gotten buck fever and started firing. Jesse Keegan didn't take a life needlessly. Abrams must have panicked for whatever reason and left men dead. Only that could rile up the community in the way Slocum had seen in the lawmen and barkeep.

"Why didn't the sheriff come after you?"

"We took to high ground. Jesse, he decoyed the posse away from us."

"Us?"

"There was another in on the robberies," Abrams said, as if the admission caused him pain. "Look, that's not important. We got to bust Jesse out soon!"

"Keegan is a friend, but I'm not going to risk my neck for friendship. I told him it was a damnfool idea coming to Idaho. He didn't listen." Slocum pushed back the chair and got to his feet.

"Slocum, wait," pleaded Abrams. "This ain't for friendship. Not entirely." Slocum glared at Abrams, waiting for the truth to finally come out.

"It's like this, see? Jesse took the gold with him. When

Morgan caught up with him, he'd hid it somewhere. He wouldn't tell the sheriff. If'n we can get him out, we can split the take. I tell you, Slocum, it's a fortune. It's more gold dust than I ever seen in my life."

"You want him out so he can tell you where he hid the gold?"

"It's more than dust! There are nuggets bigger'n your damned fist! It's a fortune, and he hid it."

Slocum wanted to spit. If Abrams had appealed to him again from camaraderie, he might have weakened. Seeing that only greed lay beneath the veneer of friendship sickened him.

"I'll think about," Slocum lied. "We can talk about it more in the morning when I've had a chance to rest up."

"Slocum!"

John Slocum spun and left the saloon, glad to be in the biting cold of the storm once more. This, at least, was honest and open. All he was likely to get from Silas Abrams was deceit.

He pulled the poncho around him, put his head down, and made his way to the stable to see how his horse was faring. He wanted to be back on the long trail for Salt Lake City at first light, if the storm let up by then.

2

John Slocum left the livery stable and started toward the boardinghouse the old man had indicated earlier. He hesitated about going in. He was cold, but he needed to pace, to walk, to take time to worry over all that Silas Abrams had said.

He didn't believe for an instant that Abrams had sent the telegram. The man's shifty eyes had told Slocum how big that lie had been. Still, who else could have sent it? Abrams had said Jesse Keegan had been on the run after escaping from Sheriff Morgan. He wasn't likely to take the time to send Slocum a wire in Salt Lake City.

"Three of them," Slocum muttered to himself. He tried licking his chapped lips and instantly regretted it. The cold wind threatened to freeze the spittle. For the end of September it was colder than a well digger's destination.

He walked the mud-and-ice streets of Idaho City, more than a hint of snow in the air again. By the time he reached the outskirts and peered back into town, the dancing snow obscured his vision. Even though the town sat in a shallow bowl, he guessed that Mount Borah was visible on a good day. But this wasn't a good day. The entire Lost Mountain Range had disappeared in the growing storm. The swirling

11

snow gave the world a fairy-tale look and hampered sound. Slocum felt as if he had been wrapped in a cold, senses-damping blanket. In this tiny bubble, he walked and thought about Keegan.

They had robbed a train or two in Utah Territory. Keegan had been a good man to have at his side. Even more than being a sensible man, Keegan knew when to take risks. Slocum hated partners who were always reckless—or always afraid of their own shadows. Jesse Keegan had balanced common sense with daring in a way that had benefited both of them.

More than once he had pulled Slocum's fat out of the fire. In return, Slocum had saved Keegan's hide. They had chosen their targets well and had always gotten away scot-free.

That had obviously changed after Keegan came up to Idaho with Silas Abrams. Keegan had met Abrams a month before leaving Salt Lake City. Slocum couldn't figure the attraction, unless Keegan was just getting bored with the Mormons and their predictable ways. The robbery Abrams described might have been daring, but it had all the earmarks of being foolhardy, too. The entire Idaho Territory swarmed with lawmen. The Nez Percé under Chief Joseph were stirring up a ruckus and keeping the cavalry on constant alert. Added to this were the numerous well-advertised gold strikes.

Mine owners tended to be lavish spenders when it came to offering rewards for those who robbed them. They might be pikers in most things, including pay to the miners, who died getting the gold ore out of the ground, but they flashed big bankrolls when it came to bringing thieves to justice.

Slocum could imagine the lure of a big gold shipment. His heart beat faster thinking about robbing such a mule-laden column or flatbed wagon breaking down under its golden load. He didn't dispute that Keegan had pulled off such a robbery. He wondered if Abrams—or the mysterious third partner—hadn't screwed up and left Keegan holding the bag. The way Abrams showed his face in Idaho City when Keegan was being locked up in the Territorial Prison at the other end of the town told who had taken the fall.

"He wants the gold, and only Keegan knows where it is," Slocum said to himself as he walked faster to keep warm. In a quirk of weather, the clouds to the distant west parted and let a ray of cold sunlight through heavy storm clouds. The snowflakes continued to fall, but Slocum was bathed in the wan light.

He didn't know if he should take this as a sign—and if he did, what it meant.

He had gone from one end of town to the other and had found only three likely-looking hotels. Slocum decided to take the stable owner up on his offer of a good meal fixed by the man's wife and possibly a warm, dry bed for the night.

For the night, only the one night, he thought over and over. Somewhere in his walk he had come to the conclusion that busting Keegan out of the Territorial Prison was too difficult a task. The weather would work against any escape. If they made it into the mountains, they might never get out alive. Cold and altitude would be more dangerous than any posse after them.

Jesse Keegan was a friend, but he had taken a different trail than John Slocum. He had chosen to come north with Abrams. Slocum decided to let Abrams get the man out, if he had the guts to try. After all, it was Abrams who stood to gain his share of the gold they had stolen and Keegan had hidden.

Even demanding an equal share, Slocum wasn't sure the risk wasn't far greater than any reward.

After retrieving his gear from the stable, he made his way up the flagstone walk to the front door of the old man's house. He rapped gently on the glass panel. The door opened almost immediately. A white-haired, matronly woman stood just inside, protected from the gusting wind by the way she held the door.

"Your husband the owner of the stable? He said I could have a place to bed down for the night."

"Come in. You must be the one Isaiah mentioned. You just rode in from the south?"

"I did, ma'am," Slocum admitted. He slipped inside. The warmth coming from the dining room and the kitchen beyond was almost painful against his flesh. He hadn't realized how close to frostbite he had come outside.

"You look a fright, sir. Come in. Would you like some supper? We're about finished, but I can scare up something."

"Thank you kindly, ma'am," Slocum said, "but I'm too tuckered out to eat much. Your husband said you served up a good breakfast. Reckon I'll need that more in the morning than I do a meal now."

"Are you sure?" she asked skeptically. "You wouldn't be putting me out none."

Slocum assured her his greatest need now was for rest, not food.

"Very well, young man. Come along and I'll show you to your room. You can settle accounts with Isaiah in the morning. No need to trouble him now." She passed a sitting room. The old man had nodded off in a large chair, his bare feet hiked up on a low ottoman in front of a crackling fire.

Slocum followed the woman up a flight of stairs and

made his way to the back of the rambling house. He wondered how they ever kept it heated during the winter—or if
they even tried. The hallway was chilly, and his room was
positively cold.

"There's a small potbelly stove you can get fired up.
Take the back stairs to the woodpile, if you like." The
white-haired woman rubbed her hands together briskly.
"You'll hardly need a fire on a night like this. It's almost
balmy."

Slocum looked at her as if she had lost her mind.

"Sir, it gets *real* cold in these parts. You get used to it or
you leave. I like it here." With that she bid him good night
and closed the door after her.

Slocum left his poncho on. He dropped his gear and
went hunting for the woodpile. The door opening onto the
stairs at the back of the house protested when he opened it;
the hinges continued to squeak as he closed it behind him.
He found the woodpile with no difficulty and hefted two
logs of about the right size to fit into the small stove. He
made his way back to his room and soon had a fire blazing.

Slocum slowly undressed. He discarded the poncho,
then climbed out of the canvas duster. In spite of two
layers of protection, snow had worked its way into his
shirt. He hung his trousers and shirt up to dry. The other
shirt he'd worn was also hung up. He crawled between the
crisp, cold sheets, still wearing his longjohns.

Memories of Jesse Keegan and what they owed each
other floated across his mind as he slipped off to sleep. He
was turning his back on a friend, but he saw no other
course of action. Keegan's troubles weren't his anymore.
They had parted company outside Salt Lake City.

Halfway through the night, the wind stopped and a
deathly silence settled on Idaho City. The cessation of the
storm brought him awake. He smiled and turned in the bed

so that his face was again toward the still-warm stove. He slipped back to sleep.

Almost.

In the stillness came deliberate, slow footsteps. He heard the back stairs protesting under a weight. The rear door rasped open on its rusty hinges. Footsteps came down the hall and paused outside his door. Slocum reached over and found the handle of his Colt Navy. The cold metal rested easily in his hand as he pulled a blanket up to cover the pistol.

He aimed directly for the door.

The door to his room opened on well-oiled hinges. A dark figure, small and bulky, filled the portal. The door closed as silently as it had opened. Only now there were two people in the room: Slocum and the mysterious intruder.

He watched the shadow moving across the room. For a moment the other man warmed his hands near the stove. Then he turned to fumble with Slocum's trousers.

The click of the Colt as it cocked sounded like mountain thunder in the small room.

"If you want to rob me, you can look in the left-front pocket," Slocum said. "You'll end up with a slug in your spine if you do, though."

The figure spun. Even though Slocum couldn't see the man's face, he knew hot guilt flushed it. The man's hands shook at being discovered.

Then he spoke.

"Mr. Slocum, I need to talk to you."

The soft, melodious voice didn't belong to any man. When his intruder lit an oil lamp and the yellow glow revealed the face, Slocum knew he was right. The woman was breathtakingly beautiful. He tried to tell himself that he had been on the trail too long, that any woman would look good to him right now.

But he knew that wasn't true.

The woman threw back her head and sent soft cascades of midnight-black hair dotted with snowflakes tumbling across her shoulders. Eyes so blue it hurt to stare at them too long boldly fixed on his green ones. She opened the heavy coat she wore. Although she wore a man's clothing, she did things for the shirt no man ever could. The bulges were exactly in proportion for a woman of her height, and the tiny waist accentuated the flaring hips clad in a pair of canvas britches.

"May I get out of the coat?" she asked, in control once more. Her hands no longer shook, and confidence filled her. Although her cheeks were flushed, Slocum thought that came from the cold night air rather than shame at being caught rifling through his trousers. "It's mighty hot in here compared to outside."

Slocum threw back the blanket and showed that he still had his six-shooter aimed at her. "Go on," he said. "Sit near the stove and warm yourself. Then you can tell me what the hell you mean sneaking into my room and trying to rob me."

"I wasn't going to rob you. I was only looking for your wallet to be sure you were John Slocum."

Slocum released the hammer on his Colt and placed it on the bed beside him. Even if she tried to get a weapon out, he could pick the pistol up and fire before she got halfway to her goal.

"How is it you know my name?"

"You were described to me," she said in a straightforward manner. "My name is Holly Hammersmith. I sent a telegram asking you to come to help Jesse Keegan."

When Silas Abrams had said the same words, Slocum

knew the man had been lying. When Holly Hammersmith spoke, a ring of truth went with them.

"What's Jesse to you?"

The additional flush that rose to her cheeks gave Slocum all the answer he really needed. Holly provided one for him, though, that verified his guess. "Jesse and I are lovers. We met here in town almost two months back."

"You're the third partner?"

She nodded, sending a tiny lock of her dark hair forward across her eyes. With a nervous twitch of her head like a frisky filly, she snapped it back into place.

"I already talked with Abrams. Why do you want Keegan sprung from the penitentiary?"

"I won't lie to you, Mr. Slocum. Jesse said you hated it when anyone lied to you. I love him, but he knows where the gold we stole is hidden. I risked my life along with them to get it. I want my share." She unbuttoned her blouse and turned slightly toward the stove, warming the bare flesh she exposed. "I also want Jesse back. We haven't been together too long, but I do love him."

"He's a cranky old bastard," Slocum said.

"He's that and more, Mr. Slocum. But I'd do anything to get him out of the prison. Anything." She turned back toward him. The last buttons on her shirt had come open. In the yellow light of the oil lamp Slocum saw the deep shadows dancing between the woman's ample breasts. A simple shrug opened the shirt even more and revealed two apple-sized breasts. Capping each was a penny-sized nipple, both erect from the cold.

Or was it only the cold that caused them to look so hard and taut and inviting?

"I checked every hotel in town before discovering you were staying here. I reckon that means you're leaving first thing in the morning and wanted to be close to your horse."

"I reckon it does," said Slocum. He couldn't take his eyes off the woman's naked breasts. Shadows played where he wanted to. A long, thin scar stretched under her left breast and intrigued him. He wanted to trace it, to find its start and its end.

She moved closer, sitting on the edge of the bed. He moved his six-shooter so it was on the bedside table.

"I got that when I was a child. My younger brother was kidding around and accidentally cut me with the tine of a hay fork." She cupped the left breast and held it out to him. "See? It's completely healed now."

"I see," he said, feeling uncomfortable. About midway down the bed, the blanket stirred and began to pulse and rise. Slocum tried to move the blanket to cover his arousal.

"Don't," Holly said softly, shucking off her shirt to stand naked to the waist in front of him. She began working on the buttons holding her canvas trousers. As she wiggled free and kicked out of her boots, Slocum knew he was going to make a very stupid decision. He shouldn't let his gonads do his thinking.

But Holly Hammersmith was so damned pretty he couldn't concentrate on anything else.

"It's getting kinda chilly," she said, shivering deliciously. "It looks a world warmer under your blanket, next to you, up close to your body."

She slipped into the bed beside him. He had no chance to say anything further. Her lips found his in a long, passionate kiss. He gasped when her fingers worked under the blanket and began working at the buttons on his longjohns. In jig time they were both naked under the blanket.

"Isn't this much better?" she whispered hotly in his ear. Sharp teeth nipped at his earlobe.

"You're trying to buy me," he accused. "You just want me to agree to bust Keegan out of the pen."

"I hope you agree," she said, "but you don't have to. Let's just enjoy each other. No strings attached. I'm here of my own free will." She giggled as she snuggled even closer to him. "Jesse didn't tell me everything about you," she said, her fingers closing around his erection. "You're bigger than I thought when I first saw you—and my imagination is pretty durn good!"

Slocum gasped again as she began stroking up and down his rigid length. He moved down a little and found those breasts that intrigued him so. He cupped the right one, taking the coppery hardness of its nipple into his mouth. He licked and kissed and sucked. The gasps of pleasure from the woman told him he was doing the proper thing.

He switched to her left and then moved lower. She released his manhood in favor of weaving her fingers through his dark hair to guide him lower. His tongue brushed across the cornsilk-soft down on her slightly domed belly, then found the thick tangle of bush just below. She moaned and sobbed as he ran his tongue across her most sensitive flesh.

She then pulled him up.

"No more," she gasped out. "Not like that. I want you inside me. I *need* it, John. Please!"

"I was never one to turn down a woman in need," he said. Her legs parted for him and he rolled atop her. His hips moved slowly until the tip of his erection found the spot where his tongue had been just seconds earlier. With a deliberate thrusting motion, he poked inside her, then stopped.

Her body shivered as if she had taken down with the ague.

"Don't torment me like this," she sobbed. "In. All the way in! I need you to make love to me, John!"

She clutched at him, her fingernails dragging along his

bare back. He jerked in surprise at the stinging. His hips rocked forward, and he sank balls-deep in her churning, moist interior. Surrounded by her clinging flesh, he almost lost control. It had been weeks since he'd been with a woman.

Holly Hammersmith made up for the dry spell.

She began rolling her hips in a circle. Slocum countered by going in the opposite direction. They worked together like a spoon in a mixing bowl, their passions merging and rising as one.

"No more," she begged of him. "Stop, no more, no more. I can't go on."

He hesitated when he heard her pleas. Holly regained her senses and cried angrily, "Don't you dare stop now! I'll have your balls for breakfast if you do!"

He laughed and began slow, deliberate thrusting. Each stroke took him farther into her body. She hunched up to meet his inward motion. Without realizing it, they strove together faster and faster. Slocum's prick felt as if it was a stick of dynamite waiting to explode—and Holly was lighting his fuse.

She tensed around him, her back arching as she bit down on her lower lip. Small sounds of intense pleasure escaped her throat and spurred him on. He kept thrusting until friction burned at his loins and lit him up like a prairie wildfire.

He spilled his seed into her clutching interior, her heels locked behind his back to make sure he didn't stray. Only after she let out a long, shuddering gasp did Holly relax her grip on him.

Spent and sweaty, they lay in each other's arms, foreheads pressed together.

"You're quite a man, John Slocum," the woman said.

"Jesse spoke highly of you, but he never mentioned this hidden talent of yours."

"No real way he could know."

Holly laughed, then kissed him impulsively. "You are real special, John." Her blue eyes bored into his very soul.

"You didn't climb into my bed just to get me to agree to getting Keegan out?" he asked.

"No," she said, and he believed her.

He cursed himself for a fool. He shouldn't say what he was going to. But he did anyway. "I'll help you get Keegan out."

Holly Hammersmith smiled, kissed him, and then began working slowly on him. A touch here, a kiss there, and he was ready once more for her. This time their lovemaking was slower, more deliberate, and even more exciting.

The third time, just before dawn, was best of all.

3

Slocum stretched in the soft, warm bed, contented thoughts floating across his mind. His eyelids shot open when he remembered how he had spent most of the night. The spot beside him in the bed was empty and cold. He sat bolt upright, trying to decide if it had been one hell of a fine dream or if Holly Hammersmith had left.

He sniffed the nippy morning air. A hint of perfume lingered. He hadn't remembered Holly wearing any, but he had been otherwise occupied. Pushing himself to the edge of the bed, he put his feet on the cold floor and shivered.

The door to his room opening caused him to grab for the Colt still resting on the nightstand.

"You surely are a nervous cuss," said Holly, slipping into the room and closing the door behind her. She carried another small log for the stove. She opened the iron door and threw the wood inside. It took her several minutes and three of Slocum's lucifers to get a cheery fire burning.

In five minutes the small bedroom had turned from freezing to bearable. Slocum took the time to dress.

Holly watched with obvious interest as he got into his trousers. She said, "I'm not holding you to any promise made while you were naked. Men see things differently when they have their pants on."

Slocum thought it over and shook his head. He'd made a promise, and he was going to keep it.

"The way it was last night was good, John," she said. "But I've got to be honest."

"We may not do it again," he finished for her.

"That's right. Jesse and I do love each other."

"He's a good man. I can understand why you'd find loving him easy."

"Loving you might be easy too, but I'm not so sure. You hold a lot back, don't you?" Those bright blue eyes of hers bored into him again, as if she saw his innermost secrets as plain as day.

"I gave my word. Keegan told you what that means."

"You never go back on it." She snorted and began pacing in the narrow space at the foot of the bed where they'd spent such a pleasurable night. Something else troubled her.

"Silas Abrams said he sent the telegram to me. I thought he was lying when he said it."

Holly's eyes widened in surprise. Then she barked out a harsh laugh. "Silas is what's gnawing away at me. Can't say he was responsible for Jesse getting caught, but he didn't go out of his way to help none, either."

"He told me about the gold, too."

Holly took a deep breath, held it for a moment, and sent Slocum's heart pounding once more at the sight of the way she filled out her shirt. She let it out in a slow release.

"You get an equal share after we get Jesse out. It's only fair."

Slocum stared out a small window at the white dusting of snow covering the yard outside. For all the howling wind and cold, he'd've thought there would be a foot or more on the ground. Autumn in Idaho was deceptive. If the weather stayed like this, they might not have any problems getting Keegan out and away from the Territorial Prison.

"Abrams is the kind who'd shoot you in the back if you gave him the chance. I've seen his kind before," said Slocum.

"I told Jesse that. He wouldn't listen. He can be real stupid at times."

"When it comes to friends, he can be downright dumb," agreed Slocum. His cool green eyes locked with Holly's blue ones. "That must be why I like him so damned much. Let's reconnoiter the prison and see how hard this is going to be."

"You want breakfast first?"

Slocum considered it. He wasn't sure how the matron who ran this boardinghouse would take it if he showed up with a young woman. Shaking his head, he said, "Let's look over the prison, then think about our bellies. There's going to be plenty of time."

"All right." Holly opened the door, looked out to be sure the hall was empty, and slipped out, heading for the back door. "You tell Mrs. Sanderson you'll be staying over a day or two and settle accounts with her. Meet me in the stable."

Slocum declined breakfast when Martha Sanderson offered it to him. The woman shook her white-haired head disapprovingly. "You're going to turn to skin and bones, mark my words. You get on back here for lunch and I'll forget you missing the oatmeal, fresh eggs, salt pork, and peach cobbler I fixed up for you." She paused and added, "You can even bring that girl with you, if you like. I reckon she's worked up a powerful appetite, even if you haven't."

Slocum tipped his hat to the woman and left, finding

Holly waiting in the stable as she'd promised.

"Nothing gets by that woman," he told Holly.

"Mrs. Sanderson is the town gossip. She's bound to know what goes on inside her own boardinghouse. Does that bother you, John?"

He remembered with delight all that had happened during the night. It didn't bother him, except for the notion that it might not happen again. He wasn't the kind to take advantage of Jesse Keegan's misfortune, not that he had the feeling he had forced Holly into anything.

Still, the lovely dark-haired woman wasn't his. She belonged to Keegan and had made this obvious.

She swung into the saddle of a small mare and reined around, waiting for Slocum to get his gelding ready for travel. He took a few minutes to be sure the old man had tended the horse properly. From all indications, Slocum had gotten his money's worth. The horse's coat looked better than it had since he'd left Salt Lake City.

As they rode, Holly talked. "I've been doing some looking into what it might take to get Jesse out." She pointed to a dilapidated wood and stone structure that had been abandoned years before. "That's the old prison."

"Looks as if they left behind a good jail," commented Slocum. He saw the iron cages rusting away through the wood walls. With a bit of work, this could have been maintained as a decent jailhouse.

If any prison could be called decent.

"Too many got away from there, especially back in '72 when the new penitentiary was getting ready to open. On Gow, one of the Chinamen convicted of murder, and Al Priest escaped. Priest was in for fifteen years for robbing the Umatilla stage. Took Sheriff Pinkham forever to catch them. They didn't want to be sent to the new Territorial Prison."

"Pinkham?"

"The local sheriff. We got lawmen coming out our ears," Holly said. "The sheriff what caught Jesse is from over in the Coeur d'Alene area. He's likely to be heading back home anytime now. But Sheriff Pinkham is local— and he's a mean one."

They rode out of town along winding roads that moved ever higher into the mountains. The road topped out and gave them a sudden view of another valley. Smack in the center of it was the new penitentiary. Slocum saw why the Chinaman and others had made their last escape tries from the other prison.

The Idaho Territorial Prison had been built in the center of a meadow, giving clear view of anyone coming or going for a mile or more. To sneak away would require a bribed guard or the best luck in the world. Slocum wasn't feeling any too lucky at the moment; he had agreed to help get Keegan out without first seeing this prison.

"The foundations are concrete. The walls are well nigh twenty feet high, and there's a couple strands of barbed wire running along the inside you can't see too well from here." Holly passed him a pair of field binoculars. He took them and scanned the terrain.

"There's no cover," he said.

"Not that I can see. The escape's got to be at night or every guard in there will know what's happening."

He saw glints of sunlight off the barbed wire—the strands that weren't rusted. Getting tangled in that dirty wire could be worse than being shot outright. Tetanus might not be as swift a killer as a bullet to the head, but it was just as certain.

"They lock up the prisoners every night at six. They never let them take off their leg irons," Holly said.

"Has anyone ever got away from here?" Slocum asked.

"Not exactly. There are escapes all the time. Most never make it out of the valley."

Slocum mumbled to himself as he studied the walls. Scaling them would be impossible unless he used grappling hooks and rope. He'd seen Indians able to climb up the sheer face of a wood wall using nothing more than two hatchets. That lay beyond his skill. Even if he did get inside, he had to get Keegan out.

"How are the prisoners treated? Do they starve them?"

"I don't know," Holly admitted. "They won't let me in to see Jesse. I've tried to talk to others inside to get a message to him, but it's like battering my head against a stone wall."

The outlook for an easy breakout slipped away. Slocum wondered how they could ever get Keegan out if they couldn't even talk to him.

"How hard is it to buy his way out?" he asked.

"The governor gives out pardons all the time. Usually, passing bogus gold dust is worth seven years. Larceny gets you a bit less. The worst is robbing gold and killing. Those are twenty years to life sentences and not many get pardoned on them."

"Who got killed?"

Holly snorted in disgust. A feather of condensation hung in the still air in front of her until she turned abruptly and fractured it. "Silas got antsy and killed two of the guards. There was no call for him to do it."

"He might just have a mean streak."

"Doesn't matter now," Holly said. "Two men died, and Jesse got sent up for it, even if he didn't pull the trigger. I'd trade Silas for him in a flash."

"The governor's not likely to let Keegan out," Slocum said, thinking out loud. "What are the chances of finding a guard and bribing him?"

Holly shrugged.

Slocum continued to study the prison. He understood why the locals thought of it with such pride. Getting in wasn't too hard. Getting out would take an act of God.

Slocum wasn't feeling too godlike right now. He had no idea how he was going to get Jesse Keegan out of this fortress of a prison.

4

Slocum and Holly Hammersmith circled the snowy valley where the Territorial Prison nestled so snugly. On foot, an escapee had no chance at all. The high, rocky walls prevented easy escape in three directions. The single road leading into the valley—Slocum started thinking of it more as a box canyon—could be blocked easily. A half-dozen guards armed with rifles might be able to seal the valley completely.

Slocum wasn't going to bet that it took any more.

And once free of the valley, the road led back toward Idaho City. The town had a reputation for getting together posses in short order. Before the federal government back in Washington started sending in cavalry to quell the Indians, vigilance committees were common. Slocum wasn't certain they were entirely a thing of the past, either.

Although Sheriff Pinkham had a reputation for being a hard-ass, some citizens viewed him as being too lenient with his prisoners. Some of his prisoners never lived to reach the tight security of the Territorial Prison. And that was considered namby-pamby.

The reconnaissance hadn't given Slocum any good ideas about reaching Jesse Keegan and getting him free. He turned back toward Idaho City with Holly at his side.

"Well, John? What do you think?" she asked after they had ridden in silence for almost ten minutes.

"I think I was a damned fool to agree to get Keegan out without looking the situation over good first," Slocum said.

"You're backing out?"

"No!" He resented her thinking he was a quitter. He wouldn't break a promise made, even if it had been when she had a distinct advantage over him. She had given him ample chance to honorably quit this mad scheme, and he hadn't taken it. He began to wonder about the ease with which she manipulated him. She was pretty, prettier than most women he'd ever seen. And she was as sharp as a whip. He pushed this out of his mind. She was all that and much more, as he'd found out the previous night, but he always made up his own mind. This time was no exception. Jesse Keegan had been a friend and deserved better than being locked up because of Silas Abrams' deeds.

"Well?"

"We're going to need help," he said. "Can we trust Abrams to get Keegan out?"

"Silas is greedy enough, and only Jesse knows where he stashed the gold."

"Abrams couldn't control himself when he started talking about the loot," said Slocum. "Is it that good?"

"It is," Holly said solemnly. "You wouldn't believe how much gold dust there was. And the nuggets were huge. Any of them would put us on easy street."

"A quarter share?" asked Slocum.

"Yes."

"What if I asked for half?" His question caused her to spin in the saddle and fix him with polar-cold blue eyes.

"To get Jesse out, I'd agree to it."

"You'd give me your share—or Jesse's?"

"Mine. His isn't mine to give away. If you want more, you'll have to make a deal with Silas and Jesse."

"I don't want more. A quarter is fine. I just wanted to be sure you were committed to this." Slocum felt better about Holly now. She wanted the gold, but it wasn't all she wanted. She'd trade everything to free Keegan.

"We need someone to find a guard to bribe. I want Abrams to do that."

"If he's caught, we've still got a chance, is that it? Can you trust him not to take the money and hightail it out of town?"

"Money?" Slocum's eyebrows shot up. "I thought you had some."

"I've got enough to keep me going. Jesse took *every-thing* when he split. I don't think Silas has any more than I do. We might be able to raise fifty dollars between us."

Slocum had about that riding in his own pocket. He hadn't thought it important to bring much—and what he had down in Utah Territory wasn't secured in any bank where he could get at it with a wire transfer. He had come by most of his money illegally. Putting it back in the very place he had robbed didn't strike him as too bright.

"Who can we buy off for a hundred dollars?" he asked.

"Not too many of the guards. They don't get paid squat, but they know what it'd mean if they got caught."

"They'd be on the inside with the prisoners they're guarding now," said Slocum.

"Convicted guards don't last long in the prison. There's been a case or two of that happening. They might last a week before someone finds them with their throat slit."

"We can talk it over with Abrams," said Slocum. "He might have a better idea than we do how to reach Keegan."

* * *

"He's honest, I tell you," insisted Silas Abrams. "I've got drunk with Gentry a dozen times. I know him."

"If he's so honest, why is he willing to talk to us about springing Jesse?" demanded Holly. The dark-haired woman stamped her foot impatiently. "I don't like this."

Slocum stood quietly outside the Mother Lode Saloon's back door. Abrams had set up this meeting with the prison guard where no one could overhear them, yet they'd have an excuse for being together if anyone chanced to see them. Slocum didn't like such meetings. Too much could go wrong. Idaho City still crawled with lawmen, even if Sheriff Morgan had gone back to Coeur d'Alene and another one had drifted home to Boise. He had seen Sheriff Pinkham up close for the first time, and he looked like one tough hombre.

"What's a woman know about things like this?" asked Abrams.

"A sight more'n you do," said Slocum. He pulled out the watch that had been left to him by his brother Robert and flipped open the case. Gentry was more than half an hour late.

"If you're getting cold feet, get on out of here," Abrams said hotly. "We don't need you."

"More'n my feet are getting cold," said Slocum. A new wind hinting at another snow-laden storm blew down from the high country. He had spent some of his money buying a decent winter coat to replace the poncho; he wished he had the battered old poncho on now too. The extra layer, even on top of the sheepskin coat, would give added warmth against the biting north wind.

Holly started at the sucking sound of boots moving in the ice and mud. Slocum half turned, hand going to his cross-draw holster and the ebony-handled six-shooter resting there. A tall, bulky man filled the mouth of the alley.

The shadow figure paused, lit a cigarette, and then came in.

From the dim illumination cast by the coal at the end of the cigarette, Slocum saw a hard-looking man with a long, waxed mustache that wiggled and twitched as the man walked. Slocum wasn't likely to make a slighting comment on the mustache, though. Gentry had the air of a killer about him.

"You the ones wantin' to palaver?" came a grating voice. "I don't like this one bit."

"We're not too happy with it, either," muttered Holly. She moved closer to Slocum, who made sure his bulky new coat hung free of his six-shooter. He wasn't expecting trouble from Gentry, but he didn't know the man or how he'd react. Anyone Abrams claimed for a friend was immediately suspect.

"Don't go listenin' to them, Gentry. This is a business deal and nothing more. I promise!"

Slocum noted the desperation in Abrams' voice. The man was uncomfortable around Gentry. And with good reason. Slocum had moved a few inches to his right to put Gentry in the center of the alley. The faint light coming from a window high up on the wall of the Mother Lode shone down on the prison guard. The large bulge at Gentry's left side came from a sawed-off shotgun hung by a thick leather strap over his shoulder.

From the way Gentry smoked the hand-rolled cigarette, Slocum guessed the man was left-handed. That deadly shotgun could be swung up and into play in a split second. The spray of lead from it could cut half a room full of men to bloody ribbons.

"You folks want to talk. Then get on with it. I got some serious drinkin' to do inside."

"We need to spring a prisoner," blurted Holly.

Gentry's eyes snapped around and fastened on the woman, as if seeing her clearly for the first time. Slocum read the man's expression and knew what was going through his mind.

Holly Hammersmith was one fine-looking woman.

"Abrams says you are amenable to making a deal," Slocum said loud enough to pull the prison guard's attention back to him. The less he looked at Holly like that, the better Slocum liked it. Holly flashed him a weak smile in way of thanks. She might have helped Keegan and Abrams with the gold robbery, but she lacked the iron core needed to stand up to Gentry.

Slocum could appreciate it. The man was like a force of nature. He stood tall and heavy, and the threat of the shotgun under his arm never went away. Gentry could turn into sudden death at any instant—and he liked for people around him to know it.

"Bustin' out a prisoner is a'gin the law," Gentry said slowly, as if the idea had never occurred to him. "A man could get ten years inside the Territorial Prison for a crime like that."

"Risk ought to be rewarded," said Slocum. He motioned for Holly to stay silent. She wanted to blather on. If she opened her mouth again, ideas might come to Gentry about what he could charge to get Jesse Keegan out. Slocum wasn't sure the dark-haired young woman wanted to pay that high a price.

The night with him had been rollicking. With Gentry, it might turn into pain.

"The risk is mighty steep. The reward would have to be . . . enticing," said Gentry.

"Can you help, if the pay is worth it?" asked Slocum.

"Reckon I kin, or find someone who is a mite more dishonest to help you. What you're askin' is for a man to break the law. Those are dangerous criminals locked up out in the valley. Turning 'em loose would set heavy on a man's conscience."

Slocum almost laughed at this. Gentry didn't have a conscience. If anything, he was no better than the men he guarded.

"What is the prison schedule like?" asked Slocum. "We need to know something about what goes on inside so we can make plans."

"That's gonna cost you too," said Gentry. "If I go shootin' off my mouth, there'll be hell to pay. I don't want to be givin' you the wrong impression."

"You want money for every tidbit, is that it?" asked Slocum. In a way, he felt better. It put their relationship with Gentry on a firm basis. Gentry got nothing unless he was paid for it, and they knew exactly what he wanted. Slocum hadn't forgotten the way the prison guard had eyed Holly.

"I'll dangle this in front of you to show that I'm willin' to cooperate—at least for the moment," said Gentry. ' We shut down at six P.M. sharp. The prisoners never have their leg irons removed, unless they're workin' on a special detail."

"Can you get anybody assigned to such a detail?" cut in Holly. Slocum wanted to push her back. She had distracted Gentry again.

"Reckon I can. I'm real important inside those tall walls. I'm what they call a shift supervisor. I say frog and they all ask how high to jump."

"A prisoner on a special detail, after six, is the best bet for escaping?" asked Slocum.

Gentry nodded. He kept his eyes on Holly.

"Can you hurry this up?" whined Silas Abrams. "It's getting cold out here."

A fresh wind blew off the mountains and formed a light layer of frost on the ground. Slocum hadn't noticed the drastic drop in temperature until Abrams mentioned it. He had been too busy watching Gentry.

"That's real good advice," said Gentry. "Let's stop beatin' around the bush and get down to what you folks are willin' to pay. First of all, I need to know who it is you're talkin' about bustin' out of the prison."

"Does it matter?" Slocum wondered if Gentry would set the price according to the severity of the prisoner's crime. More likely, he'd charge according to how much money he thought they had.

"Course it does," Gentry drawled. "I might not be too inclined to let someone I don't like get away scot-free."

"Jesse Keegan," said Slocum.

"That little weasel?" scoffed Gentry. "I'd almost be willin' to *let* him go. He's nothing inside."

"How much?"

Gentry cocked his head to one side and looked shifty. A slow smile caused the tips of his mustache to turn upward. "Three ounces of gold dust. In advance."

Slocum let out a long sigh. That was more than they had between them. He'd been hoping for Gentry to name a price in the twenty-dollar range. Three ounces of dust would buy more than Keegan's release. It was pretty nearly a king's ransom.

"That's it, then," Slocum said. He started to turn and walk off, but Holly interrupted.

"How do you plan to get him out? I want details."

Slocum saw that she was angling for a plan. It wouldn't do any of them any good—and that included Keegan.

"Around sundown things get sort of confused," said Gentry. "A man without leg irons might be standin' near the front gate and a guard like me might get confused and

leave it open a mite. What happens then is beyond my
reckoning. Why, a man escapin' like that might find a
horse outside and ride hell bent for the coast."

"See?" Silas Abrams puffed up his chest. "I told you
Gentry was our man. It's gonna be easy. Go as smooth as
silk. We'll have Jesse back 'fore we know it." He slowed
in his appreciation when the amount the guard had asked
for cooperating hit him. To Slocum, Abrams mumbled
under his breath, "Where we gettin' that kinda money?"

Slocum never had a chance to reply. The bulky prison
guard made a rude noise and started shaking his head.

"Hold on," said Gentry. "Nothing's gonna happen unless I get the three ounces of gold dust."

Slocum started to take Holly by the arm and leave. The
price was extreme for what Gentry offered. She surprised
him.

"Three ounces it is, Mr. Gentry. Here."

Holly Hammersmith fished a leather pouch from her
coat pocket and held it out to the prison guard. Slocum
wasn't sure who was the most startled, him or Gentry—or
Silas Abrams.

5

Slocum and Holly Hammersmith stared down at the Territorial Prison. Slocum shook his head. It had been three days since they had met with the prison guard. Gentry had promised them that Keegan would come running out between six and seven o'clock. Slocum had yet to see any activity near the prison gate to indicate any prisoner was allowed near enough to make a bid for freedom.

"He's taken the gold dust," Slocum decided. He turned and looked at the grief-stricken woman. The past three days had been hell for her. She had paced restlessly and had alternately fallen into moody silences and run off at the mouth.

"Silas said we could trust Gentry."

Even as she said it, the woman knew how hollow a promise it was. Silas Abrams wasn't trustworthy himself.

"He kept the gold," Slocum repeated. He stared at the squirming woman. "I've been meaning to ask you where you got the gold dust. Not an hour before that meeting you said you and Abrams didn't have fifty dollars between you."

"I . . . I had it," she said lamely. "I'm sorry, John. It wasn't that I mistrusted you. The lure of so much gold dust

41

does strange things to men. I didn't want Silas to know I had it either."

Slocum snorted. If Abrams had even a hint that Holly had squirreled away any gold dust, he'd've killed her and been off in a flash. Even if the stash Keegan had out in the mountains somewhere was as big as they'd led him to believe, Abrams would have been gone. He wasn't the type of man to trade two birds in the bush for one in the hand.

"We're not getting anywhere sitting and waiting. It's time for us to go hunting on our own."

"Gentry?" she asked.

Slocum didn't answer directly. The set to his shoulders and the grim expression were answer enough for her to know what he meant.

"This isn't right," complained Abrams. "Gentry is a fair man. He's not trying to double-cross us. I know him!"

"Shut up," Slocum said in a flat voice that was more menacing than if he'd snarled. Silas Abrams cowered into the shadows, afraid of Slocum. That suited Slocum just fine. He was tiring of this game and wanted it to be over. If it took a little bloodshed, fine. He wasn't opposed to it—as long as the blood being spilled was the lying prison guard's.

He looked across Idaho City's main street to where Holly stood hidden by the overhang of the general store. A white handkerchief fluttered into sight, then vanished.

Gentry was coming.

Slocum slipped the Colt Navy from its holster and waited. He breathed slowly, evenly, knowing this wasn't going to be an easy fight. Killing Gentry was too easy; they had to at least get the gold dust back from him.

"Gentry, look out!"

It took Slocum a split second to realize that Abrams had

betrayed him. Counting on the guard being confused at the warning, Slocum spun and swung blindly. The barrel of his six-shooter hit the burly man on the temple. The sick crunch of metal smashing into bone told that the pistol had found its target.

Gentry stumbled backward. Slocum stepped out and cocked the pistol, aiming it directly at the off-balance man.

"I just wanted to say good-bye before I blew your thieving head off."

"Wait, Slocum, don't do it!" Abrams grabbed at his arm.

This gave Gentry time enough to regain his senses and come boiling up at Slocum. Their entire plan had been to give the guard a fright and convince him it was better to cooperate than worry about being dry-gulched. Abrams had ruined everything by siding with the guard.

"You got it all wrong," Gentry said, taking the time to reach under his left arm for the shotgun slung there. He stopped when another pistol cocked loudly.

Slocum pushed Abrams away, glad that Holly had kept her head. If she hadn't come up behind Gentry and covered him with her small-caliber revolver, there would have been two bodies lying in the alley, blown apart by a sawed-off shotgun.

"You got this all wrong," Gentry said, moving his hands away from his deadly weapon. "I was looking for you folks. I wanted to tell you there's been a problem in the plan."

"What problem?" Holly Hammersmith shoved her pistol against the back of Gentry's neck. The man flinched at the touch of the cold steel that might bring instant death.

"I have to pay off two others. They changed the guard schedules. I'm not able to get to Keegan like I thought. If you want him sprung, you've got to pay them off too!"

"You lying sack of shit," Slocum said. He lifted his pistol. Again Abrams stopped him.

"We need him, Slocum. We do!"

"Killing me won't do you a damned bit of good," Gentry said. Sweat beaded his forehead. Slocum was glad to see that the man had some fear in him. He'd worried that working in the Territorial Prison had burned out all human emotion and left only a cold husk.

"It'll make me feel better. I've killed men for less. You stole our gold dust."

"No! I'm earning it. But I need more. I need at least that much more to buy off the others. It'd only be a day or two. I got to make sure of them. But I need more."

Slocum wasn't convinced. Abrams babbled how they had to trust Gentry. The deciding vote came from Holly. She moved around, her small pistol still trained on Gentry's head. Staring hard at him, she read things that Slocum missed.

"How much more gold do you need?" she asked.

"At least three ounces. Four would be better. I need to bribe two guards working near Keegan."

"All right. We'll get the gold dust. Be back here this time tomorrow night."

Gentry heaved a deep sigh of relief. He turned to go. Holly's sharp command stopped him dead in his tracks.

"Gentry, if you're not here or if you try to cross me, you'll find out what hell is like—before you die." Holly Hammersmith's determination chilled even Slocum. He had seen women in love before, but none had been this resolute.

The prison guard bobbed his head up and down and backed off. He vanished into the cold shadows. Then Slocum heard the pounding of heavy boots running.

"That put the fear into him," declared Abrams.

"I'm putting the fear into you, you sniveling slug," said Slocum, swinging Abrams around and pressing him against a wall. "You try to go against what we've planned again and I'll make sure you're dead before anything else goes sour."

"Gentlemen, let's go discuss this elsewhere," said Holly, pushing between the men. "The stable is as good a place as any." She pointed toward the boardinghouse where Slocum still slept and the small livery behind it.

Slocum stalked off, letting the others trail behind. He heard Holly talking quietly with Abrams, telling him to do as he was told. He didn't hear the man's reply.

Slocum kicked over a crate and sat on it. Holly and Abrams came in and found rude chairs of their own. In a small circle, huddling over a small coal-oil lamp Slocum had lit, they began their discussion in earnest.

"We have to trust him," said Abrams. "Gentry's not trying to do us out of more gold dust. He needs it."

"How do you know so much about a prison guard?" asked Slocum. "I've seen crooks in my day. Gentry is milking us. When we pull up dry, he'll turn us in. It's that simple."

"John might be right," said Holly, surprising Slocum with her agreement. "We don't have much choice now. We're already into Gentry for three ounces of dust. We might as well stay in the game and go for the entire pot."

"We cut our losses and run," said Slocum. "We pull back and try to figure out another way of getting Keegan free."

"Holly is right. We can trust Gentry."

Slocum studied the small, shifty creature and wondered what Jesse Keegan had ever seen in this pathetic excuse for a man. He didn't trust him, and his insistence that Gentry was doing his best turned Slocum against him even more.

"He wants more money. We don't have it," said Slocum. He looked at Holly. The woman's eyes were wide and innocent. "Do we?" he asked again, the question pointedly directed at her.

"We don't have more than what's in my pocket," she said. Slocum held his breath, almost expecting to see another pouch of gold dust thrown into the pot. Holly dropped four crumpled greenbacks. A bit more fumbling found a pair of silver dollars.

He looked at Abrams. The man swallowed hard, then began digging. He added another three dollars to their stash.

Slocum had only a twenty-dollar gold piece and six silver dollars to contribute. The rest of the money he had was in scrip and rested in his vest pocket. He wanted to hold back something if—when—this scheme went awry too.

"This is it?" asked Abrams. "This is *all* the money we have? It's not enough!"

"We've got thirty-five dollars," Holly said. "That's nowhere near enough for Gentry to use to bribe two more guards. Do we keep going or do we try to get the dust back from Gentry?"

"No!" cried Abrams. "I mean, we made a deal with him. We can't renege."

"He's already gone back on his word," pointed out Slocum. "He said he'd get Keegan out. He didn't." His cold green eyes kept Abrams silent. "We have to ask ourselves if we cut our losses and walk away or do we pony up more money. The ante is getting steep compared to our possible payoff."

"Getting Jesse out is worth any amount of money," Holly said firmly.

"Getting him out is worth it," agreed Slocum, "but it's

not worth any amount. Gentry might take us for every cent we have—and that's not very much."

"We can get more," said Abrams, his eyes darting around. When he got shifty-eyed like this, Slocum turned wary.

"What do you mean?" Holly missed the evasive way Abrams turned from them.

"We can get more money. We got till tomorrow night to scare up three or four ounces of gold dust."

"I know ways of getting that much," said Slocum, "but it takes a bit more time. We can always sift under the barroom floors for dust the miners have dropped through the cracks. There's probably five ounces in the muck under the Mother Lode Saloon's floorboards."

"That's too much like working," complained Abrams. "We're smart. We know ways to get the gold dust we need to free Jesse."

Slocum glared at the weasely man. He had suspected something like this was coming and had been resisting it. Abrams wanted to pull another robbery.

"The territory is crawling with lawmen," Slocum said. "A couple might have dropped off their prisoners for the Territorial Prison and gone home, but there are still too many around. And Sheriff Pinkham looks capable enough to form a posse and come after us, even if the others didn't want to."

"Me and Jesse pulled off a sweet robbery, Slocum. It was a damned fine one."

"I heard all about it," said Slocum. "You got buck fever and killed two guards that didn't deserve it. That's what landed Keegan in the prison."

"He—" Abrams shut up when he saw Holly's hot eyes burning into him. He averted his own eyes and shuffled one foot in the straw on the stable floor. To cover his guilt, he turned up the lantern a mite.

"*We* pulled the robbery," corrected Holly. "The three of us did it. We were partners and have to share equally, no matter what."

Slocum studied the woman's fine features in the brighter light. He found himself liking her more and more. She had screwed up on the robbery, but she was fessing up to it. Unlike Silas Abrams, she was showing some courage and character.

"Is paying off Gentry really what we want to do to get Keegan out?" Slocum looked from Holly to Abrams and back. She nodded slowly, obviously thinking about it. From all Slocum could tell, Abrams only wanted to pull another robbery.

From Abrams' eagerness, Slocum worried about a double-cross. He wouldn't put it past Abrams to take part, then dry-gulch them and make off with all the loot.

"All right," Slocum said tiredly. "We try to get the gold dust to bribe Gentry some more."

"It's for two other guards," Abrams cut in.

"Sure," said Slocum, at the end of his patience. "And Keegan is going to sprout wings and fly out."

"We have to try, John." Holly laid her hand on his arm. He held his anger at Abrams in check.

"We'll try it, but we're not going to rush into it this time. If we can't pull the robbery off to get the dust before tomorrow night, we tell Gentry to wait."

"Fine, John. I agree."

"So do I," said Abrams, bobbing his head nervously.

"I do the planning for the robbery. I say when, I say where—or even if we do it. Does anyone have any objections to that?"

No one did. Slocum pushed back and stood. He had a

great deal of scouting to do and even more planning. He wasn't sticking his head into any noose just to get Keegan out.

Slocum watched Abrams and Holly leave the stable and wondered just why the hell he *was* doing this. He returned to his small room, shaking his head and muttering to himself.

6

Slocum's fancy new sheepskin coat had a thin covering of ice on it before he returned to his room in the boardinghouse. He slunk up the back steps as if he were a robber. He didn't want to alert Martha Sanderson to his absence or the strange hours he kept this night. Too much would be happening in a few hours for her suspicions to be directed toward him. A simple word to the sheriff would put all his planning to no avail.

He quietly closed the door behind him, noticing instantly that someone had started a fire in the small metal stove. The dark shadow sitting motionless on his bed didn't startle him. He had expected company.

"Hello, Holly."

"What do you think, John? Are there any likely shipments for us to hit?" She moved closer to the stove, opened the door, and poked at the fire inside. The firelight dancing on her face turned her into some fairy-tale creature.

Slocum might say he was doing this for Jesse Keegan and their friendship. He was really risking his neck for the woman. She was beautiful, smart, everything a man could want. He pushed aside the unworthy thoughts he was having about intentionally failing to get Keegan out of the

Territorial Prison. He might end up with Holly if they failed.

But such scheming wasn't part of John Slocum's makeup. If she wanted to stay with him, she had to make the decision. Jesse Keegan didn't matter one way or the other. But the thought kept cropping up that he could stack the deck, just a little, and turn this breakout into a fiasco.

All he had to do was let Silas Abrams take a bigger part. The man's obvious greed would turn any plan into a calamity.

Slocum couldn't do that. He thought too much of Holly Hammersmith—and Jesse Keegan.

"There's a chance we might be able to do some good, but it'll require some risk."

"We've got to steal the gold, find Gentry, and pay him off, then get Jesse and hightail it out of here," she said, summarizing the problems for him.

"The robbery has to take place near Idaho City. That's our first hurdle. We don't have time to ride halfway across Idaho and find a really good shipment."

"How many are there from town?" she asked.

"Only one. It might be the last one of the year, too," he said. He looked out the tiny window at the softly falling snow. The feeling he got from this deceptively gentle snowfall was that a major storm was brewing behind it.

"The only ones likely to be shipping are the Paladin and Lucky Aces mines," she said.

"The Paladin shipped a day before I got to town," he said. "The Lucky Aces couldn't get all their gold onto that shipment. This is the tail end of their mining season. We might not be able to get much off their wagon."

"They wouldn't be shipping if they didn't have *some* gold to get to bigger banks over in Boise," said Holly.

"Four ounces of dust is all we need," said Slocum.

"There ought to be that and more. I saw the strongbox. There might be as much as five pounds of gold in it."

"I don't like putting our entire bet on this one shipment," she said. She bit at her knuckles as she thought. "Still, we need it to get Jesse out."

"The risk is just as big for a large shipment as it is for this one. Do we have to get Keegan out by depending on Gentry?"

"I don't trust him either, but there's no other easy way." The woman had made up her mind. Slocum had to make up his.

"We'll be running from the law both for the robbery and because of the jailbreak."

Holly laughed and looked strangely relieved. "Why not hang us for two crimes instead of just one? How are we going to take the shipment?"

Slocum sat beside her on the bed and pulled out the sheet of foolscap he had been making notes and maps on. He smoothed it on the blanket between them.

"This is Idaho City. The steep hill getting out of the valley the town sits in is our best bet for getting at the wagon. There's a heavy iron box bolted into the bed of the wagon."

"I've seen it. The entire wagon weighs almost half a ton, unloaded. The teams have a problem getting up the hill. But it's close to town—almost within sight."

He shrugged. "We have to take risks if we want the gold dust. The driver will whip the mules until he reaches the top of the hill. He changes teams and continues from there. We stop the wagon just before the summit."

"The mules are tired and the driver is occupied. What about guards?"

"There are usually two. This time there'll be just one." Slocum smiled crookedly. "A damn shame what happened

to him. He got some bad liquor over at the Bent Spur
Saloon. They started looking for someone right away and
found him."

"You?"

"Abrams," he said. "No one around here knows me.
Even if he is a shifty son of a bitch, Abrams is known."

"Not well enough," Holly said, smiling. "We might ac-
tually pull this off. He's riding shotgun, we're waiting.
There's not going to be any trouble getting to the gold, is
there?"

"There shouldn't be," said Slocum, still uneasy about
having Abrams fill such a vital role. The man had panicked
before and killed two guards. Slocum didn't want anything
happening to the driver, unless it was necessary.

"We take the gold and come back to Idaho City?"

"We come straight back and hide out until we can find
Gentry. We pass him the dust, and then we demand that
Keegan be released tonight."

"It's going to be a busy day," Holly said. "When does
the wagon leave?"

"A little before noon. We take it two hours later, circle
around, and get back to town by five, get Keegan out, and
hightail it in the other direction."

"We have some time," Holly said almost wistfully. She
reached out and touched his cheek. Her blue eyes closed,
and she waited for him to kiss her.

"We've got too much to do before we ride out," Slocum
said, hating himself for rejecting her overtures. "There's
more to the plan than just stopping the wagon."

"We've got to get it open," she said, her blue, blue eyes
opening and staring at him with the same sense of loss that
he felt. "Let's go find some dynamite."

* * *

"He's late," complained Holly Hammersmith. "How could the damned wagon be late? They left at noon, didn't they?"

Slocum rested against a large rock that gave him a decent view of the road winding up toward the summit. "As far as I know, they did," he answered. "Don't go getting jumpy on me. I need you to have a clear head."

"It might have been Abrams," she said. "He might have gotten into trouble. Hell, he might have got himself caught!"

Slocum almost wished that had happened. But it hadn't. The vibration through the boulder he was lounging across signaled the unseen progress of the heavy wagon and its team of eight mules. For the final time, he checked the dynamite they had stolen from the general store. He put it beside the road where he could get to it, then stopped to light a quirly. Pungent blue smoke rose as he puffed away on the cigar.

"Do you have to warn them like that, John? I thought you knew better."

"I'll need it soon," he said. "I don't want to take time to get a nice coal burning at the tip later on. We're going to be all right. Wait and see."

He hoped he sounded more confident than he really was. Trusting Abrams with any part of this robbery bothered him. The weasely man filled him with misgivings about their success.

"I see them! The wagon's coming, and Silas is riding shotgun on it!"

Slocum pulled his bandanna up so that the quirly poked out one side. He made certain his Colt Navy rode easy in the cross-draw holster and then picked up his Winchester rifle. He motioned to Holly, who scrambled up the boulder and perched on top of it, her rifle ready. He wanted her out of the way if any shooting started.

As the wagon struggled around a bend in the road, Slocum stepped out and fired into the air. The report sounded like a cannon in the still, cold Idaho mountain air.

The driver yelped and turned to his guard. Abrams slugged the man with the butt of his shotgun. Slocum cursed. Abrams was supposed to go along with the robbery, as if he were a victim and not a willing accomplice. Now he couldn't go back into Idaho City to report the crime and send the sheriff and a posse in the wrong direction.

"You idiot!" shouted Slocum, jerking down his mask and taking the quirly out of his mouth. "That wasn't according to the plan."

"He suspected," complained Abrams.

"Get out of the wagon," Slocum ordered. "We're going to blow it." He grabbed two dynamite sticks, went to the iron box bolted to the wagon bed and found the spots where the explosive would do the most good. He used the glowing coal at the end of the quirly to light the fuses. He pushed the driver off the wagon's hard seat and dragged him to cover at the side of the road.

The explosion spooked the mules. They started off with the wagon. Holly had dropped down from her spot atop the boulder and caught at their reins. She managed to quiet them enough for Slocum to get into the blown-apart wagon bed and force open the strongbox.

"How much did we get?" Abrams asked eagerly.

"Enough. Looks to be a pound of dust and another pound of nuggets." Slocum heaved a sigh. All this for two pounds of gold. It hardly seemed worth it except for what the dust would buy.

What price could he put on a friend's freedom?

"Get this loaded, Holly," he said, passing the gold to

her. She had brought their horses to the side of the wagon.
"I've got to tie up the guard and—"

Slocum's words were drowned out by the roar of
Abrams' shotgun. Slocum spun, rifle coming up. Abrams
stood over the driver's corpse.

"You shot him in cold blood!" cried Holly.

"It's better this way. He'd've ruined everything if you
left him alive."

Slocum's finger tightened on the rifle's trigger. Holly
stopped him from shooting Abrams.

"We need him, John. Please."

"Get on back to town," Slocum said between clenched
teeth. "Report the robbery. Then find Gentry and tell him
we'll meet with him at five o'clock tomorrow afternoon."

"Why not today?"

"Look at the time, you fool. The wagon was late. By
the time you get back to Idaho City, it'll be damned near
six."

"No, I'll ride and . . ." Abrams' words trailed off when
he saw that Slocum meant for him to return to town on
foot.

"Leave the shotgun. We'll get rid of it. You tell Sheriff
Pinkham whatever you want about the robbery, but get him
out here tonight."

"The gold. I want my share now."

"Tomorrow, after we see how much your friend Gentry
wants for bribing the other two guards. We might not have
much left after that."

"But—"

"Get going." Slocum lifted the rifle and held it so that a
simple movement would line its sights on Abrams' torso.
The man looked frightened—and with good cause. Slocum
was within a hair of plugging him.

"I'll do it, Slocum. Honest. Don't worry about me. I'll get Pinkham out here real quick!"

Slocum watched Silas Abrams hurry down the road, stumbling twice before he got to the bend in the winding mountain road and vanished from sight.

"He murdered an unconscious man," said Holly, stunned. "I thought he'd panicked before. I don't know what to believe now."

"He's a sniveling back-shooter," said Slocum. He'd seen more than his share of men like Abrams. If they hadn't needed him to draw away the law from Idaho City, he would have removed Abrams once and for all.

"Let's go. This . . . this is making me sick."

"We'll get to the summit, skirt the station there, and make our way around the mountain and back into Idaho City," he said. "If Abrams does any kind of job at all, the sheriff will keep on going and never think we'd doubled back."

"You'd better hide our trail good, John," she said slowly. "I don't like to think that Silas would turn us in, but he might."

"We've got the gold—and Keegan knows where the real trove is," Slocum said. "Until he can get his hands on one or the other, we're safe enough from the likes of Silas Abrams."

They walked their horses to the summit, carefully avoided the manned way station at the top, then found a rocky path leading back around toward the valley. The narrow trail had been blasted as a mining road, but the few shallow mine pits they came on were abandoned. Slocum checked the tailings and saw little to interest a serious miner. That meant they might not encounter anyone until they got back to Idaho City. That suited him just fine.

As they rode, Slocum became increasingly uneasy. It

took several minutes for him to decide it wasn't from the threat of being seen. The temperature in the pass had dropped considerably, and more than a few snowflakes had begun to fall.

"It'll cover our tracks," said Holly.

"It'll cover *us* if it turns into a full-fledged blizzard," worried Slocum. "Last night I thought it was getting mighty cold. This is even worse."

"It's still early for a real storm," Holly said, staring at the sky and the lead-heavy clouds forming above them. Even as the words came out, they seemed to freeze in the air. A powerful, frigid wind started blowing from upslope.

"We might not be able to make it back before the storm," he said.

"If we hurry, we can. It can't be more than two hours back to Idaho City."

It took them more than five hours along the narrow back road to reach the outskirts of the small town. Four inches of soft, wet white snow had fallen, and the heavy sky promised that much more before dawn.

7

John Slocum sat and stared out the window at the snow piling up by the stables. He and Holly Hammersmith had returned to the boardinghouse, then gone their separate ways. He wondered where she was staying. Thinking about her was driving him crazy, and he ought to stop. He knew that, and still he thought of her sleek, dark hair and those piercing blue eyes and the way she moved . . .

A knock on the door brought him around, hand on his six-shooter.

"Who is it?" he called out. He didn't think Sheriff Pinkham would knock if anything had gone amiss. The lawman would simply kick in the door and start shooting, just to be sure nothing went wrong with the arrest.

"This is Martha Sanderson. Are you all right, Mr. Slocum? I haven't seen you all day, and you came in early."

"I'm all right, Mrs. Sanderson," he said, putting down his pistol and going to the door. The white-haired woman stood outside, a metal tray covered with a hand-embroidered towel in her hands.

"I brought you some food, Mr. Slocum. You just haven't been eating, and I *am* a good cook. I don't know what Isaiah told you, but he's all wet."

Slocum laughed. "He hasn't said a word about your cooking. I've been occupied."

"Out carousing, unless I miss my guess," she said with mock severity. "You're just like he was at your age. Here. Eat. It'll do you a world of good. You're looking mighty peaked." She placed the tray of food on the small nightstand and left without saying anything more to him.

Slocum took a slice of crisp bacon from the tray and returned to the small window. The sun must be up by now, but he couldn't tell. The snowstorm had worsened. Wispy fingers of snow blew across the yard and drifted against the north side of buildings. From all Slocum had seen, this was going to be one bad storm.

He smiled as he thought of the robbery only three-quarters of a day back. The Lucky Aces Mine had been right sending their shipment when they had. This storm would block any heavy cargo for a week or more. If another storm followed on this one's heels, Idaho City might be socked in for the winter.

It was their bad luck that he had needed the gold they were shipping. Slocum snorted and took a sip of the hot coffee Mrs. Sanderson had brought. It burned his tongue and tasted bitter. She hadn't bothered to bring sugar or cream with it. Slocum continued to drink; he'd had worse in his day.

The snow assured that they had gotten away with the robbery. The sheriff wasn't about to try tracking in this blizzard. But the very cloak of white that had granted him a clean getaway turned the purpose of the robbery around. How were they ever going to get Jesse Keegan out of the Territorial Prison in this weather?

Slocum finished the meal and lay on the bed, his mind working hard. They had enough gold to bribe the guard again. Gentry was an unknown factor, though, and Slocum's distrust of him grew with every minute. They had to find a way to keep the prison guard from taking more of their gold dust and turning them in to the authorities for buying an escape. Whatever he decided on, it wouldn't include Silas Abrams.

That was another hombre he had come to dislike enough to put a slug in his head. He wondered what tall tale he had told the sheriff. It wasn't likely to be the one they had agreed on before the robbery. Slocum's anger mounted. Abrams had no call to kill the driver. That had been cold-blooded murder.

Still, something good had come from the murder. Slocum knew now that Abrams hadn't panicked before. He had murdered the two guards on Keegan's robbery, too.

A knock came at the door.

"Come on in," Slocum called. "It's open." He expected Mrs. Sanderson returning for the empty tray. He was delighted to see Holly Hammersmith.

Snowflakes sparkled like small jewels in her midnight-black hair. Her eyes were warm and alive and brought a warmth to the room that had been lacking. Slocum hadn't realized how much he had missed her—and they had only been apart for a few hours.

"I got the rest of what we'll need," she said, out of breath. She rubbed herself to get circulation back into cold arms. Slocum silently indicated a spot beside him on the bed. She snuggled close. The cold from her outer jacket penetrated to the bone.

"We're ready, except for one small detail," Slocum said.

Holly nodded solemnly. "How are we ever going to get in touch with Gentry?"

"He looks the type to need more than one drink a night. He might make it in to a saloon. I can check to see."

"Let Abrams do that," she said. "They seem to be asshole buddies." She hugged herself even harder.

"You're finally beginning to see what sort of snake in the grass Abrams is?" he asked. He had never heard her so down on Keegan's partner before.

"He didn't have to kill the driver," she said angrily. "I poked around town and made a few inquiries. To hear Abrams tell it, he held off damn near a hundred desperadoes. He was even calling for the town to give him a reward for what he did."

"They'd hang him from the nearest tree if they knew."

"*I* should hang him from the nearest tree," Holly grumbled. "It's because of him that Jesse is in the Territorial Prison. I've been thinking about this real hard. He and Gentry might be trying to bamboozle us."

"There's not much we can do to control Gentry," Slocum admitted. "Once he goes into the prison, he's beyond our reach. We've got to depend on someone, though. There's no other way I see to get Keegan out."

"I know." She half turned and buried her face in his chest. He felt hot, wet tears on his shirt. "I feel so damned helpless. I don't like this. I wish Jesse was already out. I wish we'd never teamed up with Abrams."

He put his finger under her quaking chin and lifted it. "What else do you wish?"

Her damp eyes closed and her lips puckered. He bent down and kissed her firmly. For a moment, the world stood still. The wind howled outside and snow continued to drift. They might be here for hours—even days. Slocum had seen his share of Canadian storms screaming down from the Yukon to know their full fury.

He was content to lie in the soft bed with a cheery, warm fire burning in the pot-bellied iron stove and wrap his arms around Holly Hammersmith.

"This might be the last time, John," she said softly.

"We're going to find Gentry, and he's going to get Jesse out, and we're going to get the hell out of Idaho."

"I know," he said. He kissed her again.

Her heavy winter coat slipped off. She didn't stop there. As if peeling an onion, she worked down through the layers of clothing she wore to keep out the winter cold. She paused for only a moment before shucking off her trousers.

Slocum had to laugh. "The longjohns look becoming on you. You fill them out nicely in all the right places." He put his hands on her buttocks and squeezed. She wiggled closer. He moved his hands along the woolens to her thighs. A quick brush between her legs made her go weak in the knees. She sagged back to the bed.

He pressed down on her breasts, still hidden behind the soft wool. Hard nipples rose up to meet his questing fingers. He teased them until he felt her pulse throbbing wildly in each of the rigid buttons of aroused flesh.

"You're overdressed for this. Let's get down to where we're both on even ground," she said. Her nimble fingers worked on his shirt, his trousers, his belt, everywhere. In less than a minute, he too was stripped down to his longjohns.

"We're a fine pair," she said.

"I see a fine pair," Slocum said, smiling. He unbuttoned the front of her longjohns and bared her chest. Dropping to his knees beside the bed, he licked and sucked at the two coppery, firm nipples he had exposed. Holly gasped as he licked across their summits, then down the slopes of her breasts.

"My turn," she said, struggling across the bed. "I see something hard and round that I want free." She grabbed him by the balls and tugged him toward her. He went willingly. She worked dexterously to skin his longjohns off until his erection throbbed long and red.

He silently stripped off her woolens. The two of them lay on the bed, naked and ready. Hands exploring constantly, they slowly aroused each other until Slocum felt as if he was going to explode like a stick of dynamite.

"Careful how you handle that," he said as she stroked up and down his rigid length. "It's all primed and ready to go off."

"The fuse is lit?" she asked, a wicked gleam in her eye. "I'd better put out the fuse."

Slocum gasped as she went down on him. Her tongue rolled around the end of his cock, making him even harder. His balls tightened until he was sure he was going to burst at the seams. Her agile fingers worked all over his groin, teasing and touching, pinching and soothing. But it was her mouth that excited him to the limits of his endurance.

"Don't do that anymore, not unless you're ready for the consequences," he gasped out.

"Why, John, you're all flushed and hot. Is the fire too hot?"

"I'll show you how hot it can get." His arms circled her and drew her close. They kissed with a fervor that he had seldom experienced. Tongues dueling, they explored each other's mouths until they were both panting.

Holly broke it off. "I need air. You're one fine kisser, Mr. Slocum."

"That's not all I do well."

"Show me," she urged.

He rolled her onto her back. Those alabaster thighs that drew him so parted and showed his amorous destination. He turned onto her and moved to position himself. He wanted to ram in hard, but he held back. Moving his hips in small circles, he teased her most sensitive flesh as she had teased him with her tongue.

"John, oh, John!" she moaned. "That's so nice. I . . . I

feel like I've got a forest fire blazing inside me. Do something. Put it out. Please!"

She clutched at him with surprising strength. He was pulled toward her belly. He felt himself slipping into a hot, wet channel that took away his control. He couldn't help himself once she surrounded him so thoroughly.

His loins aflame, he slipped balls-deep into her. For a delight-filled moment he paused to savor the sensation ripping through him. Then he pulled back, slowly, deliberating, teasing her once more. When only the purple tip of his manhood remained inside her, he paused and looked down.

A hot flush tinged her breasts, shoulders, and neck. Holly's eyes were closed, and a look of complete rapture was on her face. He had no doubt that she wanted more. He had no doubt that he was the man to give it to her.

Sliding easily back and forth, he worked slowly, easily, building tensions. Friction burned at his length as it vanished into her heated channel. Her fingers stroked over his chest and caught up tiny swirls of the hair she found. As exciting as anything he did was watching her expression as he moved with increasing speed. Every thrust caused her to tremble a bit more. The flush on her breasts and neck became more pronounced. She moaned and sobbed and uttered nonsense words as their bodies moved together.

Her hips began lifting off the bed to meet his every inward thrust. He straightened when a cold blast of air crossed his back. But nothing could stop him now. His passions had been kindled. He swung back and forth faster and faster.

"Oh, John! More! I want more!"

He gave her more than either of them could stand. His hidden length quivered and jerked harder, then erupted into her yearning cavity. Holly's legs circled his waist and pulled him into her firmer than Slocum would ever have dared.

Locked together, they rocked to and fro until their passions were spent. Sweaty, exhausted, he sank forward and took her in his arms. For a long time they lay without speaking.

Both thought the same thing: this might be the last time.

Slocum broke the silence. "There's still some coffee left. Would you like some of it?"

"Yes," she said, her eyes only for him.

He sat up in the bed and reached over to the nightstand for the coffee cup. He blinked twice before he realized the coffee cup—and the tray it was on—had vanished.

Slocum remembered the cold draft he had felt across his back. Mrs. Sanderson had entered and removed the emptied tray, and he had never noticed.

"Never mind," Holly said, pulling him back to the bed. "You're all I need. For now."

And he was.

8

"Where's the little lady?" asked Gentry. "I was kinda hankering to see her again."

"She's across the street and has a rifle sighted on your head," Slocum said evenly, enjoying the way Gentry squirmed. The guard tried not to spin around and try to find Holly; the furtive glances over his shoulder betrayed his nervousness more than if he had tried to find the would-be bushwhacker.

"I tried to tell them it wasn't necessary," said Silas Abrams. "I tried to, Mr. Gentry. Honest."

The burly prison guard glared at Slocum, then changed expression slowly until a smile blossomed like a morning glory on his face. "You don't have anything to worry over," Gentry said. "I ain't gonna steal your gold dust. This is for my friends."

Slocum looked across the street, as if checking on Holly Hammersmith. The blowing snow obscured the view. Even if she had been posted on the roof of the hotel as he had claimed, the woman couldn't have gotten a good shot. She was down the alley, hiding behind a stack of crates near the back door of the saloon. From there she had a decent shot at both Gentry and Abrams.

If it was needed, she had a good shot.

"I can still take your dust, and you can't do squat. You know that, don't you?"

"We wouldn't be here if we didn't have some trust in you," said Slocum. He ignored Abrams entirely.

"That's right touching, it is," said Gentry. "And it's not misplaced. I'll get the dust out to the two men who're gonna be on duty. You won't have any trouble getting Keegan out."

"The storm's moving in again," pointed out Slocum. "We've got to have Keegan by six o'clock."

"For this much gold, they'll deliver Keegan to you personally. Where do you want him?"

"Out the front gate will do," Slocum said dryly. He wasn't impressed with Gentry's attempts at humor. He wasn't impressed with much at all about this jailbreak. They had to play along with the guard, though, because he was their only chance of freeing Jesse Keegan before the storm came down from Canada and completely blocked all hope of escape.

"This surely does ride well in my pocket," said Gentry. "I got to get on out to the prison. Finding those boys might take a spell. They don't always come to work on time."

"Just be sure you're there—and so is Keegan."

"You're not threatening me, now, are you?" Gentry thrust out his chin and belligerently bumped into Slocum.

Slocum didn't budge an inch. The coldness in his eyes was all the answer Gentry needed. The larger man backed down, muttered to himself, and stalked off.

"I'd hate to have to hunt him down and kill him," Slocum said, sure that Gentry could hear. The words were as much for Abrams' benefit as for the prison guard's.

"You're goin' about this all wrong, Slocum," said Abrams. "You shouldn't badger him like you do."

"I'll do more than badger if he tries to cross me. You don't want me for an enemy either."

"You never liked me," whined Abrams, "since me and Jesse came north. You blame me for what happened."

Slocum said nothing. The full blame could be laid at Abrams' feet. He had butchered three men in robberies and was likely to murder even more, given the chance. Slocum intended never to turn his back on the man.

Holly came out from her hiding spot, Slocum's Winchester resting in the crook of her left arm. "How'd it go?" she asked. "I couldn't hear what was being said over the howl of the wind." The dark-haired woman shivered a little and pulled her coat more tightly around her to protect herself from the increasingly chilly wind.

"We go out in an hour," said Slocum. "Keegan will have his chains off and be let out the front gate. We have a horse waiting there, and we ride like hell."

"Then we can get the gold we took," chortled Abrams.

"Then we fight the damned storm that's coming in," said Slocum. He studied the heavy sky and knew they were enjoying a brief respite from the prior night's blizzard that had left almost a foot of new snow on the ground.

"We don't have anything to worry about," Abrams assured Holly. "Pinkham is out chasing down the robbers what killed the driver and made off with the Lucky Aces' gold. The other lawmen don't care a bucket of warm spit what happens out at the Territorial Prison. We're home free, I tell you."

Slocum was glad he and Holly had prepared for a long chase through even blizzard conditions. Their supplies were adequate for a month, if not longer. All he worried about was getting Keegan free—and Silas Abrams.

"Let's get ready," Slocum said. He had left enough scrip on the nightstand to take care of his food and lodging at

Mrs. Sanderson's. There wasn't any point in telling her he was leaving. She'd only get suspicious of someone leaving in the middle of a storm. Even this way, she'd know he had something to do with Keegan's escape. Where else would a sane man go in the middle of the season's first bad snowfall?

They rode silently up the road leading to the bowl where the Territorial Prison rested. A shroud of white covered the ground, drifting as much as two feet in places. The last vestiges of autumn had been eradicated for the season, leaving only the promise of more wintry weather to come.

"When is Gentry going to bring Jesse out?" asked Holly. "He's taking too long."

Slocum studied his watch, that ghost-legacy of his dead brother Robert. He snapped the cover shut and said, "It's time. I don't know if Gentry was bringing him out or if one of the others he's paying off will. It doesn't matter as long as we get Keegan."

Slocum stood in his stirrups and turned, studying the road behind them. "Stay here," he said to Holly.

"No!"

"You have to be lookout. We don't want a posse creeping up on our rear ends and cutting us off. There's nowhere to go if we head deeper into the canyon."

"I'll give warning," she said, mollified.

"Abrams and I can handle this," said Slocum, wondering what he was getting himself into. He signaled to Abrams to ride down on the far side of the trail leading to the prison. The growing twilight hid them from all but the most intent guard. From what Slocum had seen, the guards didn't bother looking outward too often; they watched their prisoners more closely.

Slocum and Abrams stopped a dozen paces from the main gate. There wasn't a guard on duty. Slocum pulled out his Winchester and levered a round into the chamber. They hadn't even seen Keegan, and already the plan was falling apart.

He dismounted and tethered his horse to a low hackberry bush, now devoid of all foliage and fruit after the previous night's snowstorm. Tramping through the brittle, ice-crusted snow, Slocum made his way to the tall barbedwire gate and peered inside the compound. Prisoners, their feet shackled, hobbled back and forth on their way to bed down for the night.

"I want to talk to Gentry," Slocum called out. "Is he around?" He moved the rifle so that no one inside would see it.

A passing guard turned and stared at Slocum as if he had two heads. The man hefted a Sharps .69 and walked on without saying a word. Slocum began to sweat. Nothing was going right.

He started to leave when another guard came to the gate and yelled for him to stop.

Slocum stood exposed, a dark target against the white snow. He held back the urge to lift his rifle and fire at the guard. Being this close to the Territorial Prison worked on him in ways he didn't like. He was sorry he had gotten involved with trying to get Keegan free.

"I've got something for you," the guard said. "A big package, if you know what I mean." The guard's nervousness conveyed itself to Slocum as another indication that their plan was falling apart around their ears. He wanted to call it all off, but he couldn't. He had to take the chance of getting Keegan free.

"Where is it?" Slocum asked cautiously.

"There's been some trouble," said the guard. "The other guy who was supposed to get the shackles off never showed up for work."

"Where's Gentry?"

"Not here," the guard said vaguely. "You want the package or not?"

"Yeah, send it out right now," said Slocum.

The guard fumbled at the gate and unlocked two chains and the heavy locks holding them. A dead bolt screeched free. Some other locking device protested, and then the heavy gate swung open a fraction of an inch. Slocum went to peer into the compound and saw only shadows moving in the darkness. It took him a second to realize he was staring at a man's chest.

"What'n the bloody hell are you doing here?" the guard grumbled. Slocum knew that this wasn't the man he had just exchanged pleasantries with. The guard lifted his hand to a holstered six-shooter.

Slocum reacted instinctively. He swung the butt of his Winchester around and connected squarely with the guard's chin. The man's head snapped back, and he fell like a marionette with its strings cut.

"Jesse?" Slocum called. "You there?"

"John? Is that you?" Jesse Keegan shuffled into sight, a bowl in his hand. "They were feeding us when a guard told me to come out here. What's going on?" Keegan stared at the fallen guard.

"Isn't it obvious?" snapped Slocum. "Get your ass out here. We're breaking you out!"

"We?" Keegan just stood, as if he didn't want to go anywhere. "Who else is with you? Is it Holly?" The man's face brightened. Slocum thought glumly that Holly Hammersmith could bring any man back from the dead.

"Of course it is. And Silas Abrams, too, for all the use he's been. Where's Gentry?"

"The guard? I don't know. Is he helping? He's got a

reputation for double-crossing prisoners who pay him for special privileges."

"Get out here!" Slocum took two steps into the Territorial Prison and grabbed Keegan's arm. He pulled hard, getting the man moving. Slocum had no idea how long it would be until someone noticed that the gate was open or the guard he had cold-cocked no longer was patrolling his post.

"We're really going?" Keegan appeared confused. He stumbled and fell to his knees when Slocum jerked hard to get him moving. Slocum had to pull him back to his feet and shove him toward the open gate.

They had taken too much time leaving the prison. A cry went up. Slocum spun, rifle ready. He spotted the guard who had raised the alarm. He sighted and squeezed the trigger. The Winchester barked and sent a foot-long tongue of flame into the twilight. Even faster raced a lead slug. It unerringly found its target and buried itself in the guard's chest. The alarm died—for a few seconds.

Then all hell broke loose.

From every direction came returning fire. Slocum ducked as splinters from the two-story-tall wall exploded around him. Duck-walking out of the Territorial Prison, he found Keegan struggling in the snow. The leg irons kept him from taking more than a half-step.

"Abrams!" he shouted. "Get him out of here!"

Slocum knew it wasn't smart calling out names like this, but he had no choice. Silas Abrams might not even come when he called. The man could have turned tail and run at the first shot. To Slocum's surprise, Abrams trotted over, his rifle ready. He led the horse they had brought for Jesse Keegan.

"Get on and ride," Slocum told Keegan. "Holly's waiting at the top of the rise."

Keegan was coming out of his prison-induced daze. Slocum had seen similar responses from men who had been behind bars too long. It startled him that Keegan was acting this way after barely two weeks in the Territorial Prison. Conditions inside must be terrible if Keegan's spirit had been broken this fast.

Slocum forgot all about Jesse Keegan when a fusillade of lead rained down around him. One bullet nicked him on the neck. The hot streak galvanized him into motion. Simply standing outside the prison was the quickest road to ending up inside those walls—or worse.

He began firing with measured cadence, driving back the less venturesome among the guards. A few, however, came rushing through the gate after their escaping prisoner and his allies.

Slocum coldly picked off all three. Their blood hissed and smoked as it pumped from their bodies onto the cold snow drifted by the entrance. By this time, a roar had risen inside the compound as prisoners scented freedom. Slocum hoped others would escape. They would obscure their tracks as they got out of the shallow bowl of a valley holding the prison.

He jerked when another slug ripped along his side. The stinging trail along his left ribs turned to putty and began to flow wetly inside his shirt. His longjohns soaked up some of the blood and helped the wound clot over quickly. He winced as he raced for his horse. Tiny fountains of snow erupted around him as the prison guards climbed up their towers and began firing at him.

One marksman was coming too close. Slocum whirled and dropped to a crouch, bracing his left elbow on his knee. The long knives of orange flame stabbing from the corner of the prison pinpointed his target. Slocum waited for a second shot before he squeezed the trigger. He was rewarded by a shriek of pure agony. He doubted that he had killed the other man; he had definitely put him out of commission.

"Hurry, John, don't trade yourself for me!" Jesse Keegan raced by, riding sidesaddle. His heavy leg irons clanked as the horse struggled through the foot-deep snow and up the steep slope leading out of the valley.

Slocum had no intention of taking Keegan's spot inside Idaho's Territorial Prison. He mounted and wheeled his horse around. More guards poured from inside the prison. In seconds the air filled with humming lead insects, any one of which could rob him of his life. Slocum bent over his horse and urged the gelding to its utmost. The horse responded.

From behind he heard barked commands to get horses and pursue. Slocum kept low until the words blurred and became indistinct. Only when he reached the spot where he had left Holly Hammersmith did he slow his headlong pace.

He stopped to give his horse a much-needed rest. Slocum went cold inside as he looked around. He couldn't see Holly or Keegan or even Silas Abrams. He couldn't see much beyond the end of his nose because of the white veil that had been pulled across both Territorial Prison and Idaho City.

The grandfather of all snowstorms had moved in while he was getting Keegan out of jail.

9

Slocum knew that the others must have ridden down the road toward Idaho City. Their plan had been to cut due west at the fork in the road and get the hell away from the town. Within an hour it would be boiling with angry citizens—and a posse would be forming. Sheriff Pinkham might have returned from his wild goose chase after the robbers who had killed the driver on the Lucky Aces' shipment over the mountains. If so, he would be hopping mad and less likely to ignore the townspeople's demands to bring the criminals to justice.

Any criminal.

Slocum's neck began to itch with the feel of an imaginary rope around it. They wouldn't likely wait for something as time-consuming as a trial. They'd string him up on the spot from the nearest telegraph pole. Him and Keegan and Abrams and probably even Holly.

He strained to hear in the gathering snowstorm. From the direction of the Territorial Prison came sporadic gunfire. They fired into the dark and gathering storm, hoping to stop their escapee. Slocum turned to face Idaho City. He thought he heard distant hoofbeats. It was all he had to go on. Keegan and the others must have gone that way.

Through the obscuring snow he rode hard and fast. The gelding protested his mistreatment by loudly whinnying. Slocum slowed his breakneck rush and again listened. The wind whined through the tall trees and blotted out any chance he had of following the others by the sound of their horses.

Reaching what he hoped was the fork in the road, one branch going into Idaho City and the other heading due west, Slocum pulled his sheepskin coat tighter around him and urged his horse into the white turmoil. Icy knives slashed at his cheeks. The metal on his rifle turned so cold that it stuck to his numbed fingers. He pried the weapon loose and returned it to its sheath.

Tracking in the storm was impossible. He both cursed and praised the wind blowing so strongly and the snow falling so heavily. Any posse coming after them would find it impossible to follow a track; their spoor would be blotted out instantly.

It worked against him too. He had to find Keegan, Holly, and Abrams. How he was going to do it in this storm was beyond him. All he could do was keep riding as fast as he could and hope he overtook them soon.

If he didn't, he had the scant consolation of getting Jesse Keegan out of the Territorial Prison. What he wanted now was the payoff. Holly had promised him a quarter share of the gold they had stolen earlier. He didn't even have the remaining dust and nuggets from the bloody robbery from the Lucky Aces Mine shipment. Those Holly had kept.

Eyes stinging, Slocum rode on. Less than fifteen minutes later, Slocum knew he was going to get so turned around he would never be able to find his way. He reined in. His gelding snorted long, hot plumes of breath into the cold night in way of thanking him.

"We're going to go to earth, old fella," he said, patting the horse's neck. "When this blows over, we'll find them. They can't do much traveling in a storm like this either."

Slocum's biggest worry was getting turned around and finding himself blundering along Idaho City's main street.

He found a small stand of junipers that afforded some protection from the wind and blinding snow. He led his horse into the grove and found a rocky area where he could block off most of the wind. He scouted around and even found enough dry wood to build a small fire on the lee side against a large boulder. The horse shivered but didn't protest. It stuck its nose through the snow and sought brush just under the surface. For Slocum's part, he was glad to drink a little hot coffee. It warmed him like nothing else.

He drifted off to sleep, the storm raging around him. He awoke hours later to dead calm. Slocum stared up through the limbs of the trees and saw velvet darkness and crystalline pinpoints of stars. The storm had passed over as he slept.

"Get ready to move," he urged his horse. "We're going to have a posse hot on our heels before you know it."

They found the road again, mostly by trial and error. The dirt road had vanished under six more inches of freshly fallen snow. He dug down and found frozen ruts. Squinting into the night, he found a lofty mountain shimmering like a ghost peak with a new coat of snow. Mentally tagging this as his guidepost, Slocum began riding.

As he rode, every sense strained. The unnatural silence cloaking the land was the aftermath of the storm. Nothing stirred. The wind had died. Even the mountain spirits the Nez Percé believed in had gone to sleep for the moment.

When he heard the creaking of leather tack and the protests of horses, he knew he had finally overtaken Keegan and the others. Slocum spurred his gelding on, cutting off the road and heading into the foothills.

A tiny fire with smoke curling above it confirmed his guess about locating Keegan.

Three figures huddled around the fire trying to warm their hands. Slocum decided to make it four. He rode up slowly, then called out, "Jesse, Holly, Abrams? That you?"

"Slocum?"

"Don't, Silas. Are you crazy?" came Holly's sharp command.

The rifle shot that echoed through the mountains startled Slocum. He hunkered down and then slid from horseback. He fumbled under his coat and found the Colt Navy holstered there. Taking out his rifle would be futile. He didn't know if it had frozen up on him; the six-shooter had been next to his body, and the lubricating oil on it would have stayed warm enough to allow a few shots.

"John, come on in. Silas just got a spot of buck fever— like he did before." Jesse Keegan's disgusted voice told Slocum that the escapee had been talking with Holly about all that had happened. Silas Abrams wasn't thought too highly of in Keegan's camp.

This made life a tad easier for Slocum. He didn't have to do a world of explaining that might look as if he was jealous of Abrams's friendship with Keegan.

"Put the six-shooter away," urged Keegan. The man sat near the tiny fire, his feet thrust out toward the flames. Silver nicks on his shackles showed where they had tried breaking him free with a rock. That he still wore the chains meant the citizens of Idaho Territory got their money's worth with the prison.

"I got separated in the storm," Slocum said, easing down beside Keegan. His eyes were on Abrams, though. The man turned sullenly and vanished into the night.

"Where's he going?" asked Holly. "I'll—"

"Don't," Slocum and Keegan said at the same time. They looked at each other, then laughed.

Keegan said, "We always did think alike, John. That's what made us such a good team." He spat and took a new bite from a plug of chewing tobacco they had bought for him. "That might be why I took up with Silas. We *don't* think alike. Made for a refreshing change."

"You enjoy the vacation in the Territorial Prison it got you?" asked Slocum.

"Help me with his chains," said Holly, kneeling. She clutched a rock in her bare hand, ready to pound some more on the iron links. The hand she clutched the rock with was red, and the fingertips had turned bluish.

"Put your gloves back on," said Slocum. "This is the slow way of doing it." He stepped back and aimed his Colt carefully. The first bullet whined off into the still night, barely touching the links. The second and third slugs did more damage. He checked and decided a fourth wouldn't help matters. He found a sharp-edged rock and finished the job Holly had started.

"The cuffs will take a sight more work," said Keegan, "but this is the first time I've been able to take a full stride since they put me in that hellhole."

"You can ride without looking like an Englishwoman, too," said Slocum. "Those shots might have alerted a posse, if they're after us yet."

"They will be," Keegan said. "The guards Abrams killed weren't just ordinary folks. One was the brother of the Idaho City mayor. The other had connections all the way to Boise. Never did figure out what his pull was, but the governor sent down an edict saying that if I wasn't convicted, he'd personally come on over and plug me himself."

"Friendly place, Idaho," observed Slocum. "The sooner we're out of it, the better off we're going to be." He looked at Holly, but she had her full attention on Jesse Keegan. He sighed, knowing this was the way it had to be.

"We've got to get the gold before we think about moving on," said Keegan. "That might not be too easy, since I stashed it in a place that's hard to find. And there are the Nez Percé to deal with. The talk among the guards was about how Chief Joseph was making monkeys of the cavalry. He's dancin' around 'em and causing all sorts of shit to fall on their heads."

"We can get the gold come spring," said Slocum. "Holly's got a little stored up from another robbery we did."

Keegan turned and raised his eyebrows, indicating he hadn't heard about this. Slocum wondered if Holly had kept it from Keegan intentionally or if there just hadn't been time to talk about how they'd financed his escape.

"We get the gold now," insisted Keegan. "That way we can part company with Abrams. I don't want the son of a bitch around me any more than I have to."

Slocum had to agree. He'd as soon shoot Abrams in the head and leave him for the posse. Silas Abrams was nothing but trouble waiting to happen. If they didn't back-shoot the man first, he'd do it to them, but only after he learned where Jesse Keegan had hidden the take from the earlier robbery.

Slocum started to speak to Holly when rifle fire brought him up, pistol ready. He searched the darkness for some sign of danger but didn't find it.

Another pair of quick shots from the direction Abrams had taken told him more than he wanted to know.

"A posse," Slocum said. "They made better time than

I'd've thought. Abrams is shooting at them."

"Son of a bitch," grumbled Keegan. He pushed himself to his feet and took a few tentative steps. "This is better than having the chains fastened, but I'll like it a damn sight better when those cuffs are off. They're *cold*."

"John, what are we going to do?" Holly turned to him, eyes wide. He saw no fear in those wondrous blue eyes, but there was concern. He glanced back at Keegan and knew what caused it. Jesse Keegan was hobbling, and his movements were feeble. They had starved him in the Territorial Prison.

"We run. They must have found my track in the new snow. I didn't think they'd be this quick on us."

Abrams came struggling back into the small camp through the knee-deep snow. "Sheriff," he panted. "Ten men with him. I plugged one of them. The others were too quick for me."

"You mean they didn't turn their backs for you," Holly said in a cold voice.

"There's no time for that," said Slocum. "We've got to get out of here. Where does this lead?" He pointed up the canyon Keegan had chosen for their camp.

No one knew. Slocum cursed. They might be riding into a box canyon and a trap if they took that route. But he saw no alternative. If Sheriff Pinkham and ten men were behind them, they couldn't hope to fight their way back out.

Slocum climbed into the saddle and got his horse moving through the snow. The animal labored and left a trail a blind man could follow, even in the dead of night.

"I don't like saying this, but we've got to hope for another killer of a snowstorm. We're not going to shake them off our trail any other way."

"We can ambush them," insisted Abrams. "We ride up

the canyon a ways, then wait. I can gun down two, maybe three, before they know what's hit them."

"We ride and try to outdistance them," said Keegan. "We don't have the ammo for a big fight. Do we?" He looked at Holly, who shook her head. They had enough ammunition for hunting and routine defense, but they lacked the boxes required for a full-scale battle.

Slocum and Holly rode side by side while Keegan ranged ahead. He knew the terrain the best of any of them. Abrams brought up the rear. Slocum almost wished the man would sacrifice himself to the posse. That might be the best thing that could happen. Otherwise, Slocum knew there'd be a showdown between the two of them.

If they survived.

Slocum was acutely aware of how hard the going was for their horses, and how easy tracking would be for the sheriff. He tried to think of some way of hiding their trail. There just wasn't time. The posse was too close.

"John, Holly, I found a side canyon. I seem to remember that it swings around and joins up with the main valley. There's a small river in the bottom. It's not frozen over—it can't be. The winter's not come down hard enough for that yet."

"Let's try it," said Slocum. If they could ride down the stream, they wouldn't leave telltale tracks for the posse. They might even find Lady Luck riding alongside. If the stream branched, it would split the posse into two sections.

A bullet whined through the night and tore a piece from the brim of Slocum's hat. He jerked around and fired blindly. He wanted nothing more than to slow the lawmen down. He had no hope of hitting anyone using his six-shooter.

"There, John, down there!" Holly pointed to the brisk

stream. He used his knees to guide the gelding toward the cold, running water while he reloaded. He slipped the pistol back into the cross-draw holster, knowing he shouldn't give away their position now with bright muzzle flame.

He entered the stream with Holly right behind. Slocum glanced over his shoulder and saw two dark forms trailing behind them. Keegan and Abrams had been slower getting to the promise offered by the water, but they hadn't had the goad of a bullet through the Stetson to get them moving.

They rode in silence for fifteen minutes. He heard the sheriff behind them cursing his bad luck. The lawman had to figure whether they had gone up or downstream. If they found a fork in the river, that complicated his decision. The men who had followed them downstream would have to make other decisions. Slocum knew that men under pressure tended to guess wrong.

He hoped they all had terrible judgment when it came to tracking in the dark.

He almost laughed aloud when the shallow, snow-fed river split in half, one part finding its way lower through a deep, high-walled canyon and the other trickling through a shallower U-shaped valley cut by glaciers.

"We've got 'em now," he said to Holly. She smiled, her teeth reflecting whitely in the night. They kept riding for several more minutes until Slocum reined in.

"What's wrong, John?"

"Where are Keegan and Abrams?"

"They're right behind..." Holly's voice trailed off when she saw that they weren't following them.

"They must have taken the other branch," said Slocum. "I thought they saw us but—" He cut off his speculation. Silas Abrams had been riding directly behind when they entered the river. Jesse Keegan had fallen back, bringing up the rear.

Abrams had deliberately taken the other branch of the river. Getting Keegan alone might be all it took to find out where the gold from the robbery had been hidden.

Jesse Keegan's life wasn't worth warm spit if he told Abrams where he had stashed the gold.

10

"John, where are they?" Holly Hammersmith looked around frantically. When she didn't see Keegan or Abrams, she started to wheel her horse around.

Slocum caught her arm and almost pulled her out of the saddle.

"Don't do it," he cautioned. "The sheriff is back there with a posse."

"They went down the wrong fork in the river. How could they?" She was beside herself with worry.

Slocum knew what had happened. Abrams had led Keegan astray. He considered returning, then forgot all about it. The cloudless night had again changed, turning stormy. Snow came down gently, forming a soft blanket on the ground and giving his coat a thin covering of ice. The temperature had dropped fast and was heading lower, if he was any judge. Even if the storm brewing around them didn't amount to much, returning to find the other two was out of the question.

"The posse will be at the fork by now. We're not more than ten minutes ahead of them."

"The storm will force them to go back to Idaho City,"

she said, clutching at straws. "We can't let Jesse stay with Abrams. You know what will happen."

"Keegan wasn't in too good a shape when he got out of the prison. Did he tell you what they'd done to him there?" Slocum wanted to keep Holly talking, to divert her mind from the way they edged farther downstream, away from her lover.

"He couldn't. He was so weak, John. I couldn't believe it. He had lost weight, and his mind wasn't right. He babbled. You know Jesse. He was always so precise in everything he said. He's just like you in that respect."

She muttered to herself as she rode. Slocum would have preferred silence, but he knew that somehow she had to release the worry building inside. The falling snow efficiently deadened sound beyond a few yards, so he didn't concern himself too much with this. More worrisome was finding a place to hole up while the storm ran its course.

He had explored along the Lost Mountain Range years before and knew how treacherous winters were here. One minute the sky could be clear and the night cold. The next a full-blown storm from Canada would be raging through, leaving behind a foot or more of heavy, wet snow.

He didn't want to freeze to death—or have his horse die under him. The cold water in the stream had to be taking a toll on the animal's hooves.

"There," he said, pointing up the obscured side of the canyon to a small, dark opening. "A cave. We can get inside and let the storm blow over."

"But Jesse . . ." Her words trailed off as she thought about what they could and couldn't do. Staying alive was more important than finding the others.

"The snow will cover our tracks when we leave the stream," Slocum said, keeping her occupied. "You're right about the posse. They won't keep after us if the storm looks to be a nasty one."

He had no idea what the sheriff might or might not do. To someone living in this part of the country, an early winter storm might not be that bad. Slocum had grown used to the warmer climes down in Utah. Salt Lake City got its share of snow, but nothing like that falling in a few hours in Idaho Territory.

The cave was large enough for them to lead their horses inside. Slocum fastened their reins to a rock and then went foraging for wood dry enough to burn. He found some and started a small fire banked behind rocks at the mouth of the cave. The falling snow hid the thin column of gray smoke as it rose, and the rocks screened the flames from prying eyes.

"It's a good thing I insisted on preparing for a long chase," Slocum said. He began fixing a good meal. Holly wasn't hungry, but he was. He urged her to eat, and she tried. But mostly she sat just inside the cave's mouth and stared into the whiteness masking the terrain as if she could see Jesse Keegan.

Slocum finished with the can of peaches he was eating and cleaned up. They might be here for some time. He went to the back of the cave and tended to the horses. The animals might find themselves shy on food for a while, but he could fetch them some grass from under the snow when the storm lightened.

He brushed the horses and went to get some water for them from melted snow when he paused. Something wasn't right. He opened the front of his heavy coat and drew his Colt. The metal of the barrel and cylinder was cool but not cold. He knew the trusty six-shooter would work, if he needed it.

Slocum almost called out to Holly. A sliding noise

caused him to remain silent. On cat's paws he walked toward the fire.

A man wearing a lumberjack jacket dropped into view on the other side of the fire. Slocum cocked and fired in one smooth motion. The man grunted and doubled over, clutching his belly.

"What's wrong, Jed?" came the call from outside the cave. "You plug that son of a bitch?"

"Yeah," Slocum said in a level voice. "Got 'im."

The other man didn't answer, and Slocum knew he hadn't fooled him. Dropping to his belly, Slocum waited. It took a few minutes, but the man outside the cave finally got itchy and came to see what had happened to his friend.

The sawed-off shotgun he carried blazed, both barrels cutting loose at the same instant Slocum fired. Rocks and dust filled the narrow space. For a frightening instant Slocum thought the roof might cave in on him. The dirt filtered down. Slocum lay in the cave, partially covered by the fall, and waited.

After five minutes, he wiggled forward and rolled over the first man he'd shot. Opening his coat, he found a shiny five-pointed star pinned to the man's shirt. A deputy sheriff.

Slocum heaved a deep sigh. The posse had kept after them. With Keegan in no condition to travel, had Sheriff Pinkham overtaken and recaptured his prisoner? The posse had caught up with him and Holly easily enough.

He looked out into the snowy night. All sound was muffled except for the increased howling of the wind. Frigid and from the north, it carried the promise of a deadly night to be out in the open.

Slocum checked the man who had used the shotgun and decided he was just one of the posse. He didn't wear a star. Swinging back and forth from the mouth of the cave, Slocum found where the two men had come up from the stream. They had either been lucky or had been damnably fine trackers.

Another few minutes of scouting brought him to a tall pine and Holly Hammersmith. She had been tied to the tree trunk and gagged with a dirty bandanna. Her wide eyes showed fear, then relief when she recognized Slocum.

He pulled the rag from her mouth and cautioned her to silence. She choked and then swallowed, regaining her composure. "There're two of them, John."

"Then we're all right," he said, sliding his pistol into its cross-draw holster. "I took care of both of them."

"There might be more," she said, rubbing her wrists after Slocum had cut her free. "I only saw two, but the posse—"

"Don't worry about that," he said. "These two just got lucky finding us." He thought of how easily he had dispatched them and wondered if lucky was really the word.

"That means the rest of the posse went after Jesse."

Slocum helped her up and brushed the snow from her coat. The woman surely did have a one-track mind. Together they returned to the cave. Slocum dragged the bodies out and put them under a large overhang of snow. Sooner or later the snow would get heavy and come crashing down to bury the lawmen until spring thaw. By then Slocum and Holly would either be out of the territory or dead. Either way, it didn't matter to the two corpses.

Slocum fixed more coffee and added a few branches to the cook fire. He waited until Holly had finished the cup and had stopped trembling before he spoke.

"The snow's still coming down something fierce," he said. "It wasn't anything more than luck that let those two lawmen find us."

"We've got to get to Jesse," she said firmly. He had

hoped the coffee would settle the suicidal ideas rattling around in her pretty head.

"We might get lost and freeze to death. We might even run into the rest of the posse. It's a good chance Keegan and Abrams got away. Sheriff Pinkham isn't an Indian ghost. His feet get cold just like anyone else's."

"I can follow the stream back, then go after them. You don't have to come, John. You can stay here till the weather clears."

He heaved a deep sigh of resignation. He watched the silvery daggers from his nostrils stab into the night, find the hot air rising from the campfire, and vanish instantly. Their chances of dying were greater than finding Keegan alive, he knew. Even if the two men had evaded the posse and hadn't frozen to death in the storm, Keegan's life wasn't worth two hoots and a holler if he told Abrams where the gold was hidden.

"I can't let you go out alone," he said. "We'll have to go slow. The horses won't take much more of the cold water on their hooves. Freeze their legs and we're on foot."

"We can go along the stream's bank. We're not trying to get away from the posse now," she said. "John, can you understand? I *love* Jesse."

Slocum nodded. He understood. Jesse Keegan was one hell of a lucky man.

They rode along, using the stream as a guide in the blinding snowstorm. The wind had died again and let the snow fall gently. For that Slocum was glad. He didn't need frostbitten toes and cheeks. The snow muffled their sounds and cut off any chance of the posse spotting them from more than ten yards away. Slocum had to admit, though, that it worked both ways. They might come across the posse and not know it until it was too late to run.

"Here's the branch in the stream," Holly said.

"Wait a minute." Slocum dismounted and studied the banks of the stream.

"What is it?"

"Horses. At least three, maybe more. And they don't belong to the posse. These are all unshod."

"Indians?"

"The talk back in Idaho City was about Chief Joseph and the Nez Percé giving the cavalry fits. This might mean he's somewhere nearby." Slocum shook his head. How could it get any worse for them? Posse, storm, Abrams' treachery—now an Indian band intent on killing any white man they came across.

"I don't know much about them," said Holly. From the way she strained to continue along the other branch of the stream, Slocum knew she didn't want to, either. He finished his quick scouting of the area and failed to find any indication that the posse had pursued Keegan and Abrams.

"We might have gotten lucky," he said. "The Nez Percé might have chased off the sheriff."

"Jesse can't be too far away. I feel it," she said. "The wind's blowing harder down this canyon." She turned up the collar of her coat and rode into the teeth of the gathering gale-force wind.

Slocum followed her, almost losing her in the snow. Every part of his body that could complain about the cold started doing so. Then he began to really worry. The freezing wind stopped bothering him. Tiny needles of sensation danced along his fingers and face. When even this stopped, he knew he was getting frostbite.

"Holly," he called into the wind. "We've got to stop. I can't go on much longer."

Slocum tried to smile, but his lips refused to move. Holly had stopped. He had finally convinced her of the danger. He rode up beside her and saw why she had stopped.

"A trail," she said. "Fresh. Can't be more than a few minutes old."

Slocum said nothing. The tracks were from a single horse—and they came down from the side of the valley. He turned and backtracked, knowing that anything of importance they'd find would be at the start of this trail.

A few minutes later they entered a small stand of trees that cut out some of the wind's chilling force. Snow piled against a natural fence of brush and undergrowth. A small fire had been built in the center of the copse. A horse struggled against its tether to get at the few leaves left nearby. Beside the ashes of the fire lay a motionless form wrapped in a blanket.

Slocum recognized the blanket as one they'd bought back in Idaho City. Jesse Keegan had it when they inadvertently parted company.

He dismounted and went to the fire. He couldn't tell how long ago it had burned itself out. The snow and wind turned the embers cold almost immediately. From other indications, taking snowfall into account, he guessed that they hadn't missed the solitary rider leaving the thicket by more than fifteen minutes.

"Jesse!" the woman cried. She hit the ground running, stumbled, and then crawled to the unmoving body. Holly pulled back the blanket and saw the deathly white face of her lover.

"He froze to death, Holly," Slocum said softly. He put an arm around her shoulder. "It's not that bad a death. Better than rotting in the Territorial Prison."

Her tears froze against her cheeks. Slocum wished there was more he could do to comfort her, but there wasn't.

11

Digging the grave took all Slocum's strength. The ground had yet to freeze deeper than a thin crust, but the lack of a shovel hindered him. Using a sharpened branch, he scratched and scooped until he had a satisfactory grave for his friend.

"I never thought we'd get him out so we could bury him," said Holly Hammersmith, holding back her tears. She had cried right after they'd found Jesse Keegan. Now she bottled it up inside. Slocum wasn't sure which was better for the woman.

"We couldn't know it would end like this," said Slocum, hunting for words to comfort her. "Keegan never liked being penned up. Anything's better than the Territorial Prison."

"I suppose you're right, John. But we might have bought his way out if we'd bided our time."

"There's no way of knowing that," Slocum said. He stared at the mound of dirt, now blanketed with a new fall of snow. The storm came and went fitfully, sometimes dropping snow so hard it killed all visibility and at other times giving only a light sprinkling.

The snow fluttered around weightlessly, caught on the

light breeze before coming to rest on trees and ground and rocks. It would have been beautiful except for the death it brought.

"We've got to find Abrams," said Slocum.

"The gold," muttered Holly. "He probably knows. Jesse wouldn't have died without telling someone. He wasn't the breed of man to go to his grave with that big a secret."

"He knew what Abrams had done. Do you think he'd tell him anything?"

"Yes," she said with conviction. "We'd better find him before he gets away from us."

"Is the gold that important to you?"

"It is now." Hot sparks flashed in her blue eyes. "Jesse and I worked hard for that gold. It's all I have left. I'm not giving it over to a worthless back-shooter like Silas Abrams!"

Slocum saw some justification in this. He wouldn't want Abrams to be the sole beneficiary of Keegan's trove. Abrams had caused the man to go to jail because of his brutality. The Idaho City sheriff was on the hunt for them, not only for the prison break but for the other murder of the wagon driver on the Lucky Aces Mine shipment. Sheriff Pinkham might not know they had done the crime, but if Abrams were caught he would pin the blame squarely on them.

Slocum came to the conclusion that Silas Abrams was a worthless son of a bitch. If he didn't die in the mountains, Slocum might just find it a good thing to kill him on general principles.

Slocum cast one last look at Jesse Keegan's grave. He owed Keegan something and couldn't shake the notion that Abrams might have contributed to Keegan's death.

"He didn't come back upstream—we were coming

down. That means he kept on, going away from the posse."

"Going in the same direction as the Nez Percé band," Holly mused, her mind working hard on all the details. "Do you think the Indians might have found him by now?"

"They travel faster than most white men," said Slocum. "Abrams might get lucky and avoid them. It depends on the crossing canyons farther downstream."

Holly swung into the saddle and waited for Slocum. She kept her eyes averted from Keegan's grave. Slocum wondered how long it would take her to get over the grief.

They came to the stream and turned in the direction taken by Abrams and the Indians. Slocum hoped they came to Silas Abrams first. They could deal with him. He thought there were only two or three Nez Percé in the band, but he could be wrong.

Riding in silence, they went through snow flurries and one brief burst of heavy snow. Then the Idaho mountains cleared and left the night crisp and colder than anything Slocum had believed possible. When dawn came, he was ready for the sun's warming rays.

He found himself cheated even of this simple comfort. The sun rose above the mountain peak but refused to give up any of its heat.

"John, what do you make of this?"

The woman's voice startled him. He had been drifting off, sleeping in the saddle. He came awake, staring at her. Holly's attention focused on the ground. She pointed to the stream banks. Slocum rode over and stared at what she'd found.

"You have the makings of a first-rate tracker," he told her. "This is so faint I'd've missed it completely." A hoof-print in the mud had filled with a thin layer of snow over the night. The slight depression caught the morning sun and cast a small shadow inside. This was the only hint of a track, and she had spotted it.

"Abrams?"

"It must be," said Slocum, examining the hoofprint more closely. "I see the outline of a steel shoe. One nail is coming loose. His horse is probably limping from it, too."

Slocum stayed on foot as he turned toward the snowy mountain meadow where the track led. Blowing snow had erased much of the trail, but the farther he got up into the meadow, the more recent was the trace. He cocked his head to one side and listened hard. He thought he heard a horse neighing.

Slocum shrugged open his coat and found his Colt Navy in its holster. He handed his gelding's reins to Holly and motioned for her to stay back. She might be exposed in the meadow, but this was better than mixing it up with a hidden gunman.

Lawmen from Idaho City still roamed the hills—and there were Indians around. More on Slocum's mind, Abrams might not care to split the gold with two former partners. A quick bullet would end the need to share.

Snow crunching like broken glass under his boots, Slocum advanced cautiously. He drew his six-shooter when he heard the horse jerking hard at its tether. Anyone in the small camp ahead would be warned by the animal's protests.

Using a tree trunk as cover, Slocum slipped around until he got a look into the camp. A tiny fire had burned itself out. To one side he saw a snowy hummock. On the other lay a snow-covered saddle. He didn't see Silas Abrams anywhere.

The lump moved slightly, sending a tiny avalanche down its side. Slocum drew his pistol and aimed it directly at Silas Abrams.

"Get out from there," he said loudly. The rest of the snow fell away from the lump, but Abrams didn't sit up. A faint moaning sound echoed through the tiny clearing.

Slocum advanced, wary of a trap. He got to Abrams' side before he saw the sorry condition the man was in. Abrams' face had been frostbitten. From the way he kept his hands under his armpits, his fingers might have turned to ice too.

"Slocum," he croaked out. "Help me. I hurt. All over, I hurt."

"Did Keegan tell you where the gold was hidden?"

Abrams managed to nod. His bright red nose gave some hint that he was far from dying, but Slocum knew how insidious frostbite could be. Abrams hadn't been careful enough with gloves or coat. From the lack of movement as he lay on his side, his legs might be damaged as well.

"We'll get you fixed up," Slocum promised. He left the frostbitten man and waved to Holly to come into camp.

By the time she led their horses in, Slocum had a new fire blazing. He got out the coffeepot and melted some snow to get water. The brewing coffee's aroma permeated the clearing within ten minutes.

"What about the Nez Percé?" asked Holly. "Aren't you luring them here?"

"I'm more worried about the law," Slocum said. "The Indians aren't going to stay around long. They're on their way to somewhere else. The sheriff has it in mind to find us."

"He won't find Jesse," Holly said softly. "He's beyond the reach of the law." Her jaw hardened as she looked at Silas Abrams. The man was sitting up, clutching a hot cup of the coffee but not drinking it. He was thawing out his fingers before going any further.

Of Abrams, Slocum asked, "Did Keegan tell you where the gold was hidden?"

Eyes almost lost in cold, dark pits turned from Slocum to Holly and back. Abrams nodded. His voice came out weak. He had to sip at the coffee before strength returned to it.

"Jesse told me. I don't know how the hell he did it, but it's over along the Snake River. A long way off, but he gave me good directions. He knew he had to put it where he could find it again, so he made sure it was easily located."

"Where is it?" demanded Holly.

"I'll show you. I'm not dumb. If I tell you now, you'll kill me and go get it yourself."

"You son of a bitch!" Holly raged at Abrams, rising up to strike him. Slocum stopped her, though he didn't know why.

"He upped and died on me. I didn't cause it," complained Abrams. "I didn't have anything to do with him dying. He told me about the gold just before he slipped off to sleep."

"He died in his sleep?" asked Slocum.

Abrams nodded. He finished his coffee and held out a shaking hand for more. Slocum poured.

"He didn't die in pain," said Holly, somewhat placated. The hatred in her hot blue eyes as she glared at Abrams was undeniable. Slocum wondered if her reaction would have been any different if Jesse Keegan had died in her arms. As it was, she blamed Silas Abrams for her lover's death.

"Did you see a band of Nez Percé?"

Abrams looked up, shocked. "We got Indians on our trail?" he asked. "Chief Joseph's band?"

"I don't know who they belong to, but they went down

the stream after you and Keegan. If you didn't see them, they may have kept on riding. They're probably in Canada by now."

"We got big trouble if they're after us," said Abrams. He drained the boiling hot coffee and choked on it.

"Get up and move around. Get the circulation back into your arms and legs," ordered Slocum. "We're moving on when you're able. I don't want to give the law a chance to catch up with us."

"They might have gone back to Idaho City," said Holly. "The storm looked as if it would be worse than it was." A catch came into her voice as she added, "But it was bad enough. Jesse died in it."

"The posse has got a couple goads to keep them after us," said Slocum. "They got a reputation to uphold that nobody breaks out of the Territorial Prison. And I doubt if Sheriff Pinkham is giving up too easily if there's a reward posted for Keegan."

"We probably got money on our heads too," said Abrams. He sounded better, and he flapped his arms like giant wings. Although he hobbled, he was able to walk well enough to satisfy Slocum that they should be in the saddle again.

"Let me fix some breakfast. I'm famished," said Holly.

Slocum agreed to this. He found his own stomach growling with hunger. Holly used the small fire to heat some canned beans and bacon. Slocum wolfed them down, then finished off an entire can of stewed tomatoes. He was pouring himself a second cup of coffee when he heard a twig snap.

"What was that?" He looked around. Their horses were in the opposite direction from the noise he'd heard. Snow might have caused a tree limb to break, but he hadn't heard the soft cascade of snow following such an event. The Nez

Percé wouldn't give themselves away like that.

"I didn't hear anything," said Holly.

"We've got company," he said in a low voice. "The posse's found us!"

All hell broke loose as the hidden lawmen opened fire on them.

12

"Where are they?" cried Silas Abrams. "I don't know where the bastards are!"

He had dived for cover behind his saddle. A bullet cut the top of his head and left a sluggishly flowing streak that soon interfered with his vision.

Slocum's Colt was out and firing the instant the first volley cut through the clearing. He emptied the pistol's cylinder on his way to his horse. He yanked free his Winchester and began firing with a slow, measured cadence that made it seem as if a dozen riflemen were returning fire instead of just one. Slocum heard two shouts of anger and pain; two had been winged—out of how many?

To Slocum's surprise, Holly reacted faster than Abrams. She had her small .32-caliber six-shooter out and fired wildly into the sheltering trees. She didn't hit anything, but she didn't have to. The added fire kept the posse from rushing them and pursuing what advantage they'd once had.

Slocum got the horses over to the far side of the clearing and motioned to Holly and Abrams to join him. Abrams dragged his saddle clumsily. While Slocum laid down a protecting fire, the other two saddled the man's horse.

Abrams painfully got into the saddle and sagged forward.
Slocum couldn't tell if he did this out of suffering or to
keep from being shot again.

The hammer fell with a dull click as his rifle came up
empty. He reloaded and saw the brief flash of red among
the trees. Whoever he'd shot stayed down, unmoving. Slocum wasn't sure he wanted to kill any of the pursuing
posse. It was better to wound as many as possible, forcing
them to tend to their casualties and maybe return to Idaho
City. The more dead in the posse, the more likely the sur-
vivors were to follow to the ends of the earth.

"They don't have us boxed in," said Slocum, seeing
how hard the posse was trying to outflank them. The lawmen could have caught them in a cross fire if they'd taken
their time to position themselves before opening up. "We
can get out of here. Ride, Holly, and see to Abrams. He's
in a bad way."

He spoke to empty air. The dark-haired woman had already led Abrams' horse into the trees. Seconds later he
heard the hard pounding of hooves crunching through the
snow layer. Getting away from the sheriff and his men
would be hard work. Leaving a track in the snow was
about the same as going over and telling the lawmen where
they were going.

Slocum emptied his rifle's magazine and reloaded. Before using the Winchester again, he fumbled in his saddlebags to get out his spare Colt Navy. The gun seized up on
him after two shots. The cold had taken its toll on the
sensitive mechanism. Slocum cursed his bad luck and went
back to the trusty Winchester. When he had a break, he'd
have to wipe off all the lubrication from both Colts. In
weather like this, the oil froze and jammed the cylinder and
hammer.

Slocum edged out and mounted. He kept firing awkwardly over his shoulder until his rifle came up empty again. Then Slocum substituted speed for flying lead. He followed Holly's trail easily until he came to a rocky patch where the snow hadn't stuck. He kept riding as hard as he could across the slippery area, thinking that she wouldn't have slowed yet.

He was wrong.

"John!" came the ringing cry. "Up here. Above you!"

He looked up and saw that Holly had risked finding a tiny cave to hide in. Going to earth was smarter than trying to run, he knew. They needed time to regroup, to reload and gather their wits. The sheriff wouldn't be fooled long, but if they had the high ground, they might be able to fight their way out. Slocum's idea of wounding as many as possible and forcing them to return to Idaho City still seemed their best bet.

He had gone through the war as a sniper for the Confederacy. With a Brown Bess he had been able to knock out enough Union officers, their gold braid glittering in the sun, to win more than one skirmish. An army didn't function near as well without its officers. Slocum hoped to use his talents to find Sheriff Pinkham and remove him. His deputies wouldn't be anywhere near as likely to pursue after that.

His horse stumbled repeatedly on the loose rock as he worked his way upslope. He got over the lip of the ledge just as the posse pounded into view below. He slid from the saddle and kept his horse from neighing loudly and alerting the lawmen.

"Don't," he said softly, keeping Holly from using her rifle on the men below. "Let them mill around a bit. They might ride on by and leave us alone."

She snorted her contempt for the idea. He had to agree, but it did give them time to reload and get ready for a real assault. Looking above, Slocum saw a more defensible position.

"Can we make it up there?" he asked.

Holly looked at Abrams. The man's face was drawn and as pale as death. His hands shook, and he was hardly able to ride. Slocum debated leaving Abrams and pressing on with Holly.

She saw his expression and said vehemently, "We keep him with us. He knows where the gold is."

"Is the gold worth your life?"

"It's all I have left. Without Jesse, what do I have?"

To this Slocum said nothing. She was still lost in grief over the death of her lover. Still, the woman's words stung. The time they'd spent together seemed to mean nothing to her now.

"We can defend the higher ledge. From there we can even push boulders down on them if they try scaling the cliff."

"I'll get Abrams up there. Cover us," the woman said. Slocum started to argue. Her tone of voice made it sound as if she was the one in command. He considered cutting out and leaving the woman to get the stolen gold shipment's location out of Abrams. Let them both die for their damned gold. Slocum knew no amount of the glittery metal was worth his life.

The sight of Holly Hammersmith mounting her horse, her fine legs, the firm chin and bright blue eyes and the cascade of raven's-wing-dark hair made him waver. She was one fine-looking woman, and they had spent some mighty pleasurable nights together.

He wasn't sure any woman was worth his life, but he reloaded his rifle and got ready to hold off the posse if they sighted Holly and Abrams on their way up to the higher ledge.

Slocum dropped to his belly and rested the Winchester in the crotch of a low bush. His keen eyes studied the lay of the land and found the three spots where the posse was most likely to advance on them. He could cover the gullies and not worry about them sneaking up from any other direction.

He saw the man he took to be Sheriff Pinkham riding back. They had reached the far side of the rocky area and hadn't found any tracks in the snow. Slocum guessed that Pinkham had sent scouts around the perimeter of the rock to look for tracks. When they reported back that they hadn't found any, the sheriff would look to the high ground.

Taking a deep, calming breath, John Slocum readied himself for slaughter.

The posse gathered below and spent five minutes arguing. A lone rider rejoined the group and set off a new argument. To Slocum's surprise, the sheriff and half the posse backtracked the last rider's path. Four remained at the foot of the hill Slocum defended.

From above came a tiny shower of rocks. Slocum cursed under his breath. The tiny avalanche had attracted unwanted attention from the four men below.

Slocum held off shooting. He didn't want Pinkham to return with the others. He felt confident he could hold off four men. Fending off the entire posse was beyond his ability. He didn't have enough ammo, even though he did have position on them.

The men milled about, unsure about what had caused the tiny rock fall. Finally, one started toward the spot where Slocum had begun his own ascent. Whatever the lawman saw there, he called to the others to be sure.

Slocum didn't hesitate. He waited for a relatively calm period in a bout of windy gusts, then squeezed the trigger.

The bullet flew straight to its target. The man who had found the trail threw his arms up in the air and tumbled backward off his horse.

A second shot wasn't as effective. The remaining three men had their rifles out and firing, though they didn't have a good target. Slocum bided his time, just as he had done during the War. Impatience was a worse enemy than any man he had ever faced. Only when a good shot presented itself did he fire again.

A second man yelped and clutched his belly. The wounded man lost control of his horse and was thrown. Another of the men started for his wounded companion, then stopped and stared in Slocum's direction. Indecision about risking his own life was visible, even from Slocum's lofty vantage.

"Get Pinkham . . ." came the echo from below. Slocum couldn't get a good shot at either of the two surviving posse members. They had taken cover behind rocks large enough to form mountain chains of their own.

Slocum didn't think there would be a better time to join Holly. He led his horse up the steep slope, partially hidden from below. If they had rushed him now, Slocum would have been a sitting duck. His uncanny accuracy in wounding the other two kept the posse behind their protective rocks.

"How does it look from here?" he asked Holly when he got to the upper ledge.

"We might be able to lead the horses along there, get up and over into the next valley. The going would be tough, but we can do it."

"What about Abrams?"

Holly shook her head. Slocum checked the man. His color hadn't improved. Pasty white, he sat with his back to the cliff face and stared into space.

"Does your head wound hurt much?" Slocum asked as he examined the crease. It had already clotted over, but Slocum had seen men with such minor wounds do the damnedest things.

"I won't tell you," whispered Abrams. "We all get to the gold or nobody does!"

Slocum started to tell Abrams what he could do with his treasure trove, then stopped. Getting into an argument now would accomplish nothing except wasting precious energy.

"John," called Holly. "They're coming. I count five of them."

"Damnation, the sheriff's rejoined them." Slocum ran to the rim of the ledge and peered over. He saw no fewer than six men making their way up the rocky slope on foot. Pinkham must have left the wounded members of his posse to tend the horses and brought all his able-bodied men for the assault.

"Can we stand them off?"

"Why bother?" Slocum replied. "We're not getting past them. They can starve us out if we don't do anything but a Mexican standoff. Get moving along the ledge, over the top, and down the next valley. It'll give us hours before they circle and get back on the trail. Maybe longer." Slocum entertained the faint hope that the posse didn't know these valleys too well and might take a dead end, adding hours to finding the right canyon path.

More likely, he and Holly would cross the mountain and find themselves in a box canyon leading directly into the arms of Sheriff Pinkham and the waiting posse.

"All right. We'll wait for you on top," said Holly. She glared at Abrams and added so softly Slocum almost missed it, "I wish he'd talk. He'd be buzzard meat if he'd only tell me." She hurried off and got Abrams onto horseback. She had to shift some of the supplies from his saddlebags to her own. By the time she started, Slocum had settled down and had begun firing with deadly accuracy. Two more of the posse went down. He hadn't killed them, but he had put the fear of his Winchester into them.

Slocum started looking for ways to start a rock slide. He wished he had bought a few sticks of dynamite, but he hadn't. He had used what they'd stolen from the general store on the Lucky Aces' strongbox. For a stranger to buy the explosive in a place like Idaho City would have raised suspicions. He emptied his rifle and then began working on a large rock, wedging a long tree branch under the boulder.

Putting his back into the task, he started the heavy stone rocking back and forth. At the farthest point of the swing, he heaved with all his might. The boulder crunched into smaller stones, then began its slow journey downhill. As if it had been dipped in molasses, the rock turned over and over. Then it began to pick up speed and carry smaller rocks with it.

Slocum felt no sense of victory when the stony avalanche tore through the posse. He vaulted onto his horse and started after Holly and Abrams.

Halfway to the top, he heard an agonized shriek of an animal in pain. He looked up and saw Holly's horse bouncing off the side of the mountain. The frightened horse caromed past him and slid on its side through a rockfall of jagged-edged flint pieces. The shredded and bloody horse crashed to a halt a hundred feet under Slocum. Hot blood hissed into the snow and turned it red.

Slocum looked from the dead horse to the heights and yelled, "Holly!"

He got no answer.

13

John Slocum urged his horse to even greater speed, but he had to go carefully or he'd end up sliding down the sheer face of the mountain too. He couldn't keep from looking down now and then to where Holly's horse lay motionless. Already carrion birds dived down to pick at the carcass.

"She wasn't on the horse," he told himself over and over. "I'd've seen her. She wasn't on the damned horse."

Slocum knew Holly Hammersmith hadn't been astride the animal. But darker thoughts came to him. Silas Abrams might have bushwhacked her. He expected to find the woman's body at any point along the narrow ledge twisting its way to the summit.

His horse snorted and wheezed and finally reached the crest. From here he had a great view of the Lost Mountain Range and Mount Borah. He hardly noticed them. Peering back down the steep slope he saw Sheriff Pinkham's posse struggling in disarray. He took cold comfort in their trouble with the avalanche.

"John!"

He spun, hand flashing to his pistol. He fumbled as he reached under the heavy coat and touched the six-shooter's ebony handle.

"Holly?"

"Over here. I'm all right. What about the sheriff?"

Slocum eased back when he saw Holly standing over Abrams. The man was flat on his back, staring at the intense blue sky dotted with white clouds. Slocum hesitated a moment, decided the movement near Abrams' hand came from the brisk wind whipping across the mountaintop, then settled down.

"What happened?"

"My horse slipped. I was leading her, and she lost her footing on a rocky patch. I tried to save her." Holly's voice almost cracked with strain. "All our supplies were on her. I lightened the load on Abrams' horse to get him up here."

Slocum cursed to himself. In his saddlebags he had a goodly amount of food—for himself. For three the stash was not enough to keep them going for more than a week. Even rationing wasn't likely to stretch it out more than two. As worked up as the Idaho City sheriff was to catch them, two weeks hardly seemed long enough to run.

"Maybe he'll quit when he discovers there are only three of us," suggested Holly, when Slocum told her of his concern.

"He'd as soon spit in his grandmother's eye as to give up now. I think we've stung his pride. A posse out for revenge isn't going to quit until everyone's strung up from a telegraph pole."

He rubbed his neck, then stopped the gesture. It didn't do to dwell on such morbid thoughts. They were hours ahead of the posse, maybe a day or more. He had to turn that into freedom.

"How's Abrams?"

"We're not leaving him, John." The edge in Holly's voice convinced him that he might as well shoot her as leave Abrams behind. "He knows where the gold is."

"To hell with the gold. You can't spend it if you're inside the Territorial Prison—or dead."

"I want it. Jesse left it for me. I *earned* it, John."

"You stole it. You can find another gold shipment come spring. It doesn't make any sense letting him slow us." Slocum had no use for Abrams. The man was a back-shooting son of a bitch. If either Slocum or Holly had been injured, Silas Abrams wouldn't have blinked an eye when it came to abandoning them.

Slocum reconsidered. Abrams might sing a different tune if Holly knew where the gold was. Slocum looked over at the dark-haired woman and shook his head. She wasn't going to abandon Abrams until she learned where Jesse Keegan had hidden their gold. Abrams would have thought the same way, had their roles been reversed. Was the woman much different from Abrams?

Slocum hoped so, but she had changed and nowadays showed little humanitarian feelings toward Abrams. Pure greed drove her now that Keegan was dead.

Simply choosing his own trail and leaving the two crossed Slocum's mind. He forgot the notion when he studied Holly a bit more. The sunlight caught her fine cheekbones and turned her into an angel come to earth. Wind whipped her hair into a fine black net that rippled like a garrison flag. And her wide-set, intelligent blue eyes flashed with energy and determination. He didn't much like what was driving her, but he looked at her and remembered a different woman. Keegan's death so soon after his escape had upset her, and she hadn't had proper time to grieve for him.

Not with a posse hell-bent on hanging them so close on their heels.

"We've got to get moving. Can he take it?"

"Riding with him will be hard. He drifts in and out."

"You take his horse," said Slocum. He heaved Abrams across his own saddle. The gelding complained, then neighed loudly when Slocum swung up. The horse was tired, and the added weight made riding along the steep, stony mountain paths treacherous, but Slocum saw no other choice. Holly climbed onto Abrams's horse and quickly joined him.

"Let me take some of the supplies off your horse," she said. "It'll lighten the load."

Slocum started to protest, then agreed. He saw no good reason to distrust her. She hadn't tried to betray him—and he remembered how he had felt when her horse tumbled down the side of the mountain. The thought of losing Holly had troubled him more than he cared to admit, even to himself.

"It'll be fine, John. Please, trust me." She reached over and touched his cheek with her gloved hand.

"Let's go," he said, wheeling around and starting down the path on the far side of the mountain. The peaceful valley in front of them promised some measure of security. He lost the tracing of the canyon as it wound around back into the range, but he thought it formed a crossing canyon. They wouldn't be trapped in any box canyon, of that he was certain.

Abrams protested weakly and occasionally told Slocum of his determination not to reveal where Keegan had hidden the gold until all three of them were able to reach the cave.

Slocum said nothing but put the small bits of information about the gold's hiding place away in his mind. A cave. Red noses. Something about a bend in a river. Other meaningless clues were tossed out, but Slocum had the impression Abrams was recovering enough to realize he had been babbling and wanted to muddy the waters.

Slocum had to dismount and lead his horse several times down the precipitous track. As he pioneered the trail, he kept looking over his shoulder at Holly Hammersmith. She rode with her mouth set into a thin line of grim determination. He wondered what thoughts were going through her mind. If they played their cards right, she could ride away from the posse and no one would be the wiser. That required a sight more faith than she was willing to give, though.

He had no choice but to play it by ear. Slocum wanted a cut of the gold hoard Jesse Keegan had put away, but he wasn't going to risk being caught by the bloodthirsty sheriff. No amount of gold was worth spending the next seven years in the Idaho Territorial Prison.

Slocum laughed bitterly. He would never reach the prison. The posse would string him up when they came to a tree tall enough. People had died, people important to the members of the posse. He had winged a few of them in his futile attempts to make them return to Idaho City. They might be the most dangerous ones in the sheriff's rabble. They'd see themselves as having been humiliated. Revenge would be the sweeter on their tongues.

Two hours after starting down the trail, Slocum reached the canyon bottom. He considered a quick dash back down toward the stream and losing the sheriff's trackers that way. He gave it up when he heard the sound of struggling horses on the crisp, clear autumn air. The crunching of snow under hooves and the occasional cursing of the men riding the horses told him the posse had circled the mountain and were working damned hard to catch up.

"They went around rather than following us," said Slocum. "They know this country better than I do. It's taking us too long to get away compared to the way they're traveling."

"We are not giving up," Holly said almost primly. "We're going on until there's no life left in our bodies."

Her fine words meant little to Silas Abrams. The man sat astride Slocum's gelding, eyes focused ahead. Some color had returned to his cheeks, but he still looked more dead than alive. Steam jetted from his nostrils in short, ragged gusts. Other than these small signs, Slocum would have called the man dead.

"Let's not stand around lallygagging, then," said Slocum. "From the top of the hill I saw a crossing canyon. If we get to it, we can give them fits."

Holly rode alongside but said nothing. Lost in her own world, the woman neither needed nor gave any support in their mad dash to escape the posse. Slocum concentrated on keeping his horse on level terrain. The struggling gelding couldn't be expected to maintain the pace he set for long, not with two men astride.

"They don't know we're down off the mountain yet," Slocum decided, speaking more to hear his own voice than to inform Holly of the obvious. "That might keep them back for a while."

He knew that the first one to find their tracks in the new snow would bring the rest after them like a pack of hounds on a rabbit's spoor. Slocum tried urging his horse to greater speed, but the gelding refused.

They came to the crossing canyon. Slocum studied the snow-covered land and slowly worked out a plan. A mistake meant he and Holly and Abrams would end up dead. If he didn't try, their chances were even slimmer.

"Ride on up that canyon," he told Holly. "Take Abrams with you. I'll catch up later."

"But John," she protested, "they'll split up and follow both trails. What'll we gain?"

"You keep riding and let me worry about that."

"You're hoping that only a couple follow you and that you can ambush them," she said. Holly chewed on her lower lip. "That's dangerous. You might end up with more following you than come after us."

"There aren't more than six in good shape," Slocum said. "I'm hoping there are less. If there are five of them on our trail, three's the most I'm likely to face."

"I don't like it." Concern crossed her face. Then she slumped. "I don't see any way around it."

"They'll be wary of an ambush," Slocum said. "I'm hoping that will slow them a mite and give us both a better chance."

Holly nodded briskly, then wheeled around and rode up beside him. They awkwardly got Abrams onto her horse. The smaller horse staggered slightly. Slocum knew Holly wouldn't be able to make much speed with the double burden. She gave him a quick kiss, a fleeting brush of her lips on his. Then she rode off without a word.

He watched her until she vanished behind a tumble of rocks. Slocum heaved a sigh. He ought to ride like hell away from her and let the woman fend for herself. But he couldn't. He checked his Winchester and decided he was as ready as he'd ever get.

He put his spurs to the gelding. The horse shot off, grateful for the lightened load on its back. The gelding slowed quickly, though, still tired from the weight it had carried from the mountaintop.

Slocum looked around and tried to find a decent spot for an ambush. He couldn't. The meadowlands were snowy and would hold a track a blind man could follow. The canyon sides widened and left less and less chance for crawling up and firing down on his pursuers. He kept riding until he came to the crossing canyon he had seen.

A slow smile came to John Slocum's lips. A horse had

passed by recently—within the last hour, if he read the tracks right. This was the diversion he needed to confuse the sheriff and even the odds. Slocum kept riding along the canyon, circled, and came up in a small stand of trees, rifle in hand. He squatted down and patiently waited for the posse to show up.

To his surprise he had less than ten minutes to wait. Sheriff Pinkham had been closer than he'd thought. Slocum readied his rifle, studying how the three men rode. The man in the lead was obviously the sheriff. The sunlight glinting off his badge left no doubt about the man's identity. That there were two others with him meant that Holly might not have but a pair from the posse on her trail. Slocum had confidence in the woman's ability to keep away from them.

Slocum cursed when the sheriff came to the tracks and looked at them from horseback. All three men turned to the right and followed the other rider. Slocum had hoped to get at least one and possibly two of them before they returned fire.

New opportunities opened to him now, though. He might be able to backtrack and come up behind the two men on Holly's trail. They'd be easy pickings for him.

Or he could follow the sheriff and try to eliminate half of the able-bodied men still hunting him like an animal.

Swinging back into the saddle, Slocum followed the three men. He had no idea whose track they were following, but it would keep them occupied until he came within range.

He had decided the sheriff would never leave the trail until he was stopped—permanently.

Slocum caught them and pulled up, watching as the sheriff and his two cohorts dismounted and approached their quarry on foot. Curious, Slocum dismounted some distance away and cautiously advanced to see who the law-men had cornered.

"Son of a bitch!" came the loud cry from ahead. "It's one of Chief Joseph's braves!"

Slocum hurried to a spot that gave him fair cover and a good shot at the deputy who had called out. He squeezed the trigger of his rifle. The loud report echoed along the canyon walls and brought down loose snow from nearby tree limbs.

It also loosed a fusillade of hot lead from the sheriff and the surviving deputy. Slocum dived for cover, then realized they weren't shooting at him. The Nez Percé brave they had trapped was the object of their deadly wrath.

Slocum smiled as he sighted in on the second deputy. He only winged the man.

"Damn it, Sheriff, there's a whole tribe of the red-skinned bastards out there. We can't fight the entire Nez Percé nation!"

Sheriff Pinkham's head popped up from behind a low rock. Slocum took the man's hat off with his well-aimed shot. This set the sheriff and the wounded deputy into motion. They ran for their lives, going deeper down the canyon and away from the track Slocum had to take to get back to Holly Hammersmith.

He turned to leave—and found himself staring down the half-inch-wide bore of a Sharps buffalo rifle.

14

Slocum forced himself to look past the huge-bored rifle and along its battered barrel to the man holding the weapon. The Nez Percé brave was decked out in full war paint.

"You killed the lawmen," the brave said. "Why do you do this for me?"

"I did it for myself. They were after me." Slocum saw no reason to lie. He started to stand, only to be pushed back to the ground by the heavy barrel.

"The cavalry chases me. I was cut off from the others of my tribe. I am Nez Percé!" the brave cried proudly.

"Seems I solved both our problems. I'm John Slocum."

The brave's cold dark eyes bored into him. Without a word, the Indian backed away, then turned and ran lightly into a stand of trees. A few seconds later he emerged on horseback, leading a second horse with the body of another Nez Percé brave tied across its back. Slocum watched as the two, the living and the dead, vanished down the canyon in the direction taken by the fleeing sheriff.

Slocum heaved to his feet and brushed off the snow. He didn't bother checking the man he had killed. From all he'd seen, Sheriff Pinkham wasn't likely to have left a wounded man behind. He'd sooner go down shooting than to let a friend be captured by the Nez Percé.

Or John Slocum.

He wasted no time getting back to his horse and backtracking to the junction of the canyons where he had parted from Holly Hammersmith. Dropping to the ground, Slocum studied the spoor and decided that five men were tracking her. He rocked back on his haunches and wondered about the large number chasing Holly.

"Wounded," he said to himself. "The men I wounded are still chasing us."

He took little consolation in that. He hadn't winged them sufficiently to force them to return to Idaho City. If anything, they'd be madder than wet hens at the pain they'd had to endure in the hunt. Slocum patted his horse, then swung into the saddle. He had his work cut out for him.

It took the better part of the day to catch up with the stragglers in the posse. They hadn't caught Holly yet. For that Slocum breathed a silent prayer. This wild-ass scheme of his might really work, given a brush with Lady Luck.

"Down there!" he shouted, waving wildly. "I see 'em down there."

"But Len's on their trail," protested the hindmost rider. "He'd've noticed if they'd gone in that direction. Hell, that leads back to Idaho City!"

"There they are! I see them!" Slocum prodded his tired horse into a gallop until he was out of sight. He counted on the posse being worn down and not questioning who was riding up from behind making wild claims. They might think he was part of reinforcements from town—or they might not think at all.

He didn't care. He had lured three of the five off Holly's trail. Two were wounded, and the third rode as if his butt was killing him. Slocum watched from a wooded area as they vanished from sight. He backtracked again and found the trail.

Holly had stopped two miles off, her horse unable to carry both her and Abrams. She stood with her hands held high, defiantly facing her two captors.

"Go on," she said. "Shoot me where I stand, you thieving bastards. I don't care."

"Shit, Len, it's a woman," complained the man peering down the barrel of a rusty rifle. "We got the wrong ones."

"She's part of the gang," the one named Len declared. "I recognize the other one. Ain't he the guy who was on the Lucky Aces shipment a few days back?"

"Silas is his name. Don't rightly remember the rest," his companion said.

Slocum dismounted and left his grateful horse to graze at the tops of grass poking through the hard crust of snow. He drew his Colt Navy. He didn't trust his rifle since using it. It badly needed cleaning. Having it blow up in his face because of mud in the barrel wasn't to his liking.

The trusty Colt rested reassuringly in his hand as he walked up behind Len.

Holly's eyes widened slightly. This should have tipped off the two lawmen. They were too busy worrying over what capturing her and Silas really meant.

Slocum slugged Len, seeing him as the leader. It took the other man a few seconds to realize his friend was no longer standing. He swung his rifle around—too late. Slocum slammed the barrel of his six-shooter alongside the man's head. His eyes rolled up in his head, and he collapsed bonelessly.

"John! I was so worried when they caught us. Are you all right?"

Holly threw her arms around Slocum's neck and kissed

him passionately. He pushed her back and stared into her bright blue eyes. He saw relief there, but he also saw real desire at seeing him again. This was more like the reaction he expected from the woman. Their time together back in the city *did* mean something.

"Tie them up. I don't have the stomach to kill them in cold blood," Slocum said, indicating the two from the posse. He checked Silas Abrams. The man's color was better and his eyes tracked, but when he tried to speak, only a bull-throated croak came out.

"He's getting stronger," said Holly, working on bits of rope she cut from a lariat on one of the men's horses. Slocum studied the mounts and smiled. They had four horses now for the three of them—and much-needed supplies. The posse hadn't ridden out of Idaho City on the spur of the moment. They had taken time to prepare for a long, cold hunt.

"Take their coats," came Abrams' words. "Let the sons of bitches freeze out here. Serves them right."

"He's getting back to his former self," Slocum said, glaring at Abrams. He checked the ropes on the two men, then helped Abrams into the saddle of the larger horse they'd just stolen.

"What about the spare horse?" asked Holly.

"We can take turns on it. That ought to speed us up. One horse can rest while we're riding the other three." He quickly explained about Sheriff Pinkham, the Nez Percé brave, and the certainty of facing both cavalry and posse.

"It gets worse by the minute," Holly said. She grinned suddenly. "This makes you feel alive, doesn't it?"

Her smile was infectious. Slocum returned it. "Let's get moving. I want to put as many miles between us and the sheriff as I can."

Slocum guided them up the canyon, then over a crossing valley with gently sloping, bowl-like sides. He considered trying to get to the canyon rim, then forgot about it. The snow had been kicked up by dozens of horses passing recently. If they made a run for the high ground, they'd be seen by . . . who?

A close examination of the tracks showed both shod and unshod horses.

"So both cavalry and Indians have come by since the last snowfall." Holly settled down in her saddle, thinking hard on this. "Which way were they headed?"

"Hard to tell," Slocum admitted, "but it looks as if they went to the northwest from here." He pointed up a branching valley with a small stream gurgling up it. Everywhere he turned in the snowy glare, he found sluggishly flowing water. In another month—or less—every open patch of water would be iced over.

"The Snake River," Silas Abrams said unexpectedly. "That's where Jesse hid the gold."

"The Snake? But that's miles from here. How did he get over there to bury the gold?" asked Holly.

"All I know is what he told me. Which way is the Snake?"

Slocum hesitated to answer. If they went directly to the huge river, they had to take the same path already ridden by both Nez Percé and cavalry. The small pause told Holly where they must go.

She silently turned her horse and started out. Slocum followed, trying to find a bright spot in this situation. The only thing he could come up with was the mingling of their tracks with those of the other two parties. If Pinkham came this far, he'd have a devil of a time deciding where to go.

They rode until the sun dipped behind tall peaks and the temperature dropped like a hot stone in butter. Slocum reluctantly built a cooking fire, aware that the night had eyes. The cavalry might not arrest them, but the Nez Percé would lift their scalps. They were whites in a land Chief Joseph had claimed for his tribe.

Slocum tossed and turned all night, and got even less sleep when Holly came to him silently. She pressed her cold body against him. He wrapped her in his arms and she immediately slept peacefully. He lay awake much of the night gazing at the cold, hard blue-white stars above. Dawn found him aching and tired.

"The Snake is where we'll get rich," said Abrams. The man's condition had improved markedly after a good night's sleep. For once, Slocum envied him. "We'll get the gold, split it, and then go our separate ways. Agreed?"

Slocum and Holly exchanged glances, then nodded. Abrams seemed satisfied with the arrangement. Slocum wasn't sure about Holly. When Abrams had spoken, her face had gone completely blank. She would have made a hell of a poker player, he decided. But what thoughts did she hide behind the façade? He couldn't begin to guess.

"I hear water," she said, cocking her head to one side. "The Snake?"

"We're still too far south for that. A tributary might flow from here," guessed Slocum. He strained to hear the faint watery sounds. He froze inside when he heard other noises, ones he recognized all too well.

"Cavalry!" he cried. "Get mounted. We've got to get away. An entire company is coming back down the canyon."

"How can you tell?" Holly stared at him as if he had grown wings and was going to fly to the moon.

"The jangle of their harnesses. A sound that might have been the bugler signaling the rear echelons of the troop. The sound of their horses. Listen, damn it!"

"I don't hear anything," she said.

"I do," said Abrams. "Slocum's right. There's at least twenty troopers riding down on us."

Silas Abrams showed an amazing amount of strength for someone who had been so close to death the day before. He had two horses saddled in the time it took Slocum and Holly to cinch up theirs. They mounted and rode across the valley, trying to stay on rocky areas and keep their tracks in the foot-deep snow to a minimum.

"They'll see us," muttered Slocum, more to himself than the others. "They can't miss our camp. Chief Joseph gave them the slip, so they're doubling back—and we're what they found."

"How can you be so sure?" asked Holly. "They might ride on by. They might be returning to their garrison. Fort—" Her words died in her throat when she saw the line of blue-clad troopers. Their quarry was apparent.

"They're on to our trail. Damn!" Silas Abrams whipped his horse and raced off.

"He's spooked," said Holly. "They can't know we're here."

Even as she spoke, the line of troopers wheeled and started for them.

"It's almost as if they were hunting us," Slocum said, wishing for a spyglass. A civilian rode at the head of the column. The commanding officer of such a troop seldom allowed such familiarity unless it was a law officer.

"We can't let Abrams put too much distance between us. We need him to tell us where the gold is, John." Holly spurred her horse and raced after the fleeing outlaw. Slocum didn't hesitate joining her in flight. The cavalry came directly up the slope toward them. Outrunning them was their only chance for escape. All the subterfuges he had used before wouldn't work against such a well-armed, numerous band of trained soldiers.

He caught up with Holly and shouted, "That's the sheriff with them. I know it. He's got them looking for us as well as the Indians. Who knows what reward might be on our heads. Prison breaks are serious business."

"We can outrun them. They're tired. They must be. We've had an entire night to rest up," called Holly from her straining horse. Slocum saw the animal weakening already. Racing in the altitude and cold sapped a horse's strength fast—almost as fast as it did from a human.

Eyes streaming from the cold wind blowing in his face, Slocum blinked and got a good look at where Silas Abrams was headed.

"Abrams, no!" Slocum yelled. His words vanished in the whistle of wind.

The other man was racing for a frozen river. Holly began shouting too. Their combined cries for Abrams to stop failed. The man rode directly across the icy patch.

Slocum saw cracks forming with every step taken by the horse. Abrams realized his danger too late. He had ridden onto an iced-over river. If he had done it a month later, the ice would have been thick enough to support the weight of a horse and rider.

The cracks began spreading. The horse panicked and threw Abrams. He hit the slick surface and slid. A wet hole opened in the ice and swallowed the horse as it tried to reach the far side of the river. Abrams got his feet under him and took two steps before the ice cracked like a gunshot.

He vanished from sight into the freezing river.

15

"The column of cavalry? Where are they?" he called to Holly Hammersmith.

"I don't know, John," came the answer. "But Silas is dead. The water is too cold for him to have lived more than a few seconds. All that gold is lost." She turned her blue eyes toward the far side of the Snake River's icy tributary, appraising her chances of reaching it before the pursuing cavalry reached the riverbanks.

"Try to get to the other side. Dismount. Walk across slowly. Do it. I'm going after Abrams."

"John, you can't! You'll die too!"

He handed her the reins of his horse and stepped onto the shattered ice. Watery fingers reached up and took his boot heels. Slocum tried not to think of plunging into the deadly water just fractions of an inch under his feet. He walked with a deliberate gait toward the spot where Abrams had vanished from sight. When he got close enough, he dropped onto his belly and crawled.

"Abrams, can you hear me? Are you there?"

Slocum didn't have much hope of finding the man. He might have fallen straight into the frigid water and died. If the river's current under the ice was very strong, Silas

Abrams would be pinned in a watery grave until the spring thaws.

"Slocum!" came the faint cry. "Help me. I can't move. My legs are gone. My body's turning to stone. So tired. Can't hang on."

Slocum wiggled precariously close to the edge of the thin ice. Razor-sharp bits snapped free and vanished into the whirling arctic vortex where Abrams had plunged. For a few seconds, Slocum didn't see the other man. Then Abrams' hand came through the ice and grasped weakly for purchase.

Slocum made a mad grab and caught the frozen wrist and tugged for all he was worth. He almost followed Abrams into the deadly river. Only by kicking and poking holes in the ice so that his toes gave him some leverage was he able to pull the man free.

Abrams flopped onto his back like a trout on a riverbank. The man gasped for air. His face was deathly white, and frost clung to his gray-white skin everywhere. Slocum brushed off some of it. Tiny vents of steam from the man's nostrils showed that a tiny spark of life remained in his body.

"John, I see the cavalry. They're almost on top of us!" Holly gestured toward the shore at Slocum's back. He pushed the frozen Silas Abrams ahead of him like he would have a sled with runners. Abrams stirred a little, moaned, then stopped struggling.

Slocum skirted the fields of cracks in the ice, trying to stay on the thicker portions. Too many times the ice crunched under his feet and threatened to plunge him into the lethal river. Slocum changed his tactics and started dragging Abrams behind him. Progress was no faster since he slipped and slid on the ice.

"John, hurry. The cavalry!"

He looked over his shoulder and saw the officer—a lieutenant by the look of his gold braid—motioning to a squad. The civilian riding with the column argued with the officer. Slocum saw that the officer was paying little attention. He was too intent on getting his men down to the river's edge and seeing what was going on.

Slocum worked even harder to get Abrams to the far side where Holly waited for them.

"No," he ordered when he saw she that intended to come out and help. "Stay on the bank. There's nothing you can do to help either of us." Even as he spoke, he knew there was one thing that might allow them to escape.

He kept pulling on Abrams' frozen collar until he was within easy reach of the muddy bank. He let Holly tug at the man and get him all the way onto the shore while he fetched his rifle. He hadn't had time to clean it, and the barrel might be plugged with mud. Slocum took the chance. He had no other choice.

Aiming carefully at the edge of the break in the ice, he fired. The bullet ricocheted off the hard ice—and sent new cracks arrowing through the frozen expanse.

A cavalry sergeant yelled at him. Slocum kept firing. The break in the icy covering on the river spread, slowly at first, then with a speed that took Slocum's breath away. When the strong current just under the ice caught the jagged pieces, it tumbled them around and speeded up the destruction.

Sounds louder than any cannon filled the air as heavy ice floes formed and banged against each other. Before, crossing the river had been stupid. Now it was suicidal. The sergeant yelled obscenities at Slocum. Slocum waved back and then helped Holly get Abrams belly-down over the back of their spare horse.

"We've got to get as far into the mountains as possible,"

Slocum said. "It won't take them long to find another place to ford the river or a spot where the ice is thick enough to hold their horses."

"I don't know," Holly said, looking back at the treacherous river. "That's pretty fast-moving water. The ice was just on the edge of hardening for the winter. Not now. They'll have to go miles out of their way to catch up with us."

Slocum said nothing as they rode. He didn't doubt that the cavalry officer would do just that, especially if the lawman with him insisted. Nez Percé or outlaws, it hardly mattered who the cavalry troopers caught. Either would give them a bonus of returning to the warmth and comfort of their fort.

"John," Holly said after they'd ridden steadily for almost an hour. "We've got to stop. I don't think Abrams is alive."

"I checked him a while back. He's all right." In spite of this, Slocum reined back and went to check the nearly frozen man. He shook his head. Holly was right. Almost. What life had returned to Silas Abrams before his plunge into the river had been chilled out of him.

"He's getting gangrene in his fingers," Slocum said. "I reckon his toes are about gone, too. Hell, most of his body is frozen."

"Slocum . . ." The cry for help faded away as Abrams stirred on the saddle. He fought weakly.

"We'll help you," promised Holly. She dismounted and helped Slocum get the frozen man to the ground. "We'll pitch camp here and get a fire going and thaw you out."

"Warm. I need something to drink. So cold inside."

"Coffee?" Holly arched one eyebrow as she asked the question. Slocum saw that she was more interested in the coffee for herself than for Abrams. Hot water would do for the injured man. Slocum knew a dying man when he saw one.

"The posse is still after us—and so is a cavalry detachment," he told her. "We can't afford to make a fire. We can't afford to slow down, much less stop for the day."

The sun beat down on them from directly above, forcing them to squint. For all the light, Slocum felt none of the usual warmth from the sun. Winter in Idaho conspired to make life as harsh as possible for them.

"I know it's only noon," she said, "but he's dying. The least we can do is let him go with his boots off."

Slocum had to use his knife to cut the boots off, and then he succeeded only because they put Abrams's feet to the fire. Slocum jerked the man's bare feet away from the flames when he saw the flesh beginning to char; Abrams never noticed. The lower half of his body was frozen and gone.

And the upper half was in scarcely better condition.

Slocum scouted the area in the late afternoon, worrying about being found by posse, cavalry, or Nez Percé. It was as if they were alone in the Lost Mountain Range. No other human was visible, no matter where he looked or how carefully he sought out signs of pursuit. Standing on a small rise gave him a view that was unsurpassed. Snow caused him to squint, but the view was worth it.

Stretching in all directions were mountains clad in the purple of distance-haze. White ice clouds formed herring-bone patterns across a sky so blue it made Slocum's heart ache. The storms of the prior days had vanished. Only a hint of darkness showed along the rim of mountains to the north, and Slocum dismissed this as a trick of vision. From his vantage point he felt like king of the world.

Holly Hammersmith calling to him brought him down from his solitary, majestic perch.

"John, I don't think he's going to make it. Silas is dying by inches."

Slocum knelt beside Abrams and checked his pulse. At first he thought the woman was wrong, that Abrams had already died. Then he picked up a thin, thready pulse that hardly showed any life remaining. He propped up Abrams's head and tried to look into the man's eyes. His eyelids fluttered, but the eyes behind refused to focus.

"How are you feeling?" Slocum asked.

Abrams rocked his head from side to side. The eyes snapped into focus on Slocum. A weak voice said, "Can't feel anything. Warm all over. My toes tingle. Somebody's sticking needles into them. Tell them to stop."

"He's hallucinating," Holly said softly.

"There's not anything we can do for him," admitted Slocum. "He isn't feeling anything below the waist. Look." He pulled back the blanket over Abrams. Holly gasped.

"I knew it was bad, but not that bad." She looked away. To her credit, she didn't puke her guts out, although Slocum wouldn't have blamed her much. The sight of a man rotting away wasn't pretty. The icy plunge had frozen Abrams. Circulation had never returned to the destroyed limbs. Now that gangrene had set in, poisons were pumping through the rest of the man's body.

Putrefaction would kill Silas Abrams long before the dawn came.

"Did you see any cavalry?" she asked, changing the subject of Abrams's imminent death. Slocum put his arm around her and pulled her close. She snuggled against his frosty coat and ran her hands beneath it for warmth. He didn't protest when he felt her icy fingers against his bare chest.

"They had to go at least a mile upriver to cross over. We

started a regular spring thaw along the river. It's still early in the season. We were lucky to get across like we did."

"They won't stop hunting us, will they?"

He held her closer. "That depends on the Nez Percé. If Chief Joseph makes his presence known to them, the cavalry will go after him. No sheriff is going to dictate to the U.S. Cavalry."

"The posse's gone back to Idaho City?"

He had no way of telling. Sheriff Pinkham was a man with a wild hair up his ass. He wasn't going to let any escapee ride out of Idaho Territory. By the time he had found the two posse members tied up, he'd be putting different facts together in his head.

Slocum hadn't made a secret of his presence in Idaho City. Vanishing when he did made him a prime suspect as an accomplice in Jesse Keegan's prison escape. A few questions would tie him to Holly Hammersmith. Mrs. Sanderson was the center for gossip in the town. And it didn't take a mental giant to connect Silas Abrams to both of them. Pinkham would figure out what had happened to the Lucky Aces gold shipment and put himself in line for a rich reward from the mine owners.

All he had to do was bring back Holly, Abrams, Keegan—and John Slocum.

He and Holly sat staring into the banked campfire until only embers remained. A stiff wind from the north kicked up that worried Slocum. The hint of moisture carried a long way on the chilling breeze. Another potent Canadian storm was brewing. Their supplies had been reduced drastically when Holly's horse had taken the tumble down the mountainside. They still had enough to get out of the mountains. Beyond that, Slocum wasn't sure.

Another blizzard would strain their resources to the limit.

"Slocum," moaned Abrams. "Need to talk to you. Man to man."

"What is it?" Slocum dropped to his knees beside the man.

"I want it straight. I'm not going to make it, am I?"

"No."

Silas Abrams heaved a sigh that ended up a cough that wracked his entire body. He couldn't even roll to his side to clear his throat by spitting.

"Want to tell you what Keegan told me."

"The gold?" cried Holly Hammersmith. She pushed Slocum aside and pushed her ear down close to Abrams' mouth to hear his weak whisper better. "Where is it? What did Jesse say?"

Slocum saw the change in the woman once more. Greed had replaced love. He didn't doubt she had loved Jesse Keegan. Now she loved the thought of gold more than she did the man's memory.

Abrams looked from Holly to Slocum. To Slocum he said, "Got to get it soon. Up high. Near the Snake River. At noon a tree casts a cross shadow on the right place."

"Where do we have to stand to see it?" demanded Holly.

Slocum knew the gold had been hidden in a cave; Abrams had already revealed this during his feverish ranting.

"Where along the Snake do we see the cross pattern?"

"An oxbow. Right in the bend. Red rocks. Under her nose. Right under her nose."

"What are you talking about, Silas? Under whose nose?" Holly shook him to get the answer. She was shaking a corpse.

16

"He didn't tell me a damned thing!" shrieked Holly Hammersmith. "The son of a bitch died without telling me where Jesse hid the gold. How dare he?"

"He's dead," Slocum said, pulling her away from Abrams. "There's nothing more you can do to make him talk."

"All that gold," she moaned, sitting with her head resting on her bent knees. "We risked our lives for it—Jesse died!—and it's all lost."

"We can put him into a cave," Slocum said, staring at the lifeless Abrams. "Come springtime he might provide a decent meal for some roving animal."

"Let him rot here, for all I care. He didn't tell me where the gold was. I've gone through all this, and what do I have to show for it?" She hissed like a cat. "The sheriff is after me. The cavalry is hunting me down. Jesse is dead. And I'm a pauper!"

"You've still got some of the gold from the Lucky Aces robbery," Slocum pointed out. He knew she had less than two ounces of gold left after bribing Gentry and his good-for-nothing guard friends. If Holly had a bitch coming, it was against the guards in the Territorial Prison. They didn't stay bought.

"Two ounces compared with fifty pounds of gold? John, this is El Dorado. This is the treasure trove of a lifetime. I could have lived like a queen in San Francisco on that much gold. I could have been a *lady*!"

He didn't bother telling her it took more than money to make someone a lady. He silently dragged Abrams' body away from their nearly dead fire and left it in the snowy bushes at the edge of the campsite. He stared at the frozen cadaver and wondered what it would be like splitting fifty pounds of gold with Holly Hammersmith. That much gold could make living a sight easier for a long time. It had also brought about the death of a close friend and his partner in the robbery. Slocum didn't bother counting the guards at the prison who might have died, or those in the posse. They had taken their chances and had lost.

He wasn't a loser. And he knew more about the location of the gold than Holly did. He had listened carefully to everything Abrams had muttered after they'd lost Holly's horse. He hadn't known about the oxbow bend in the Snake River before. That wouldn't make finding the gold much easier, but it verified a definite location once the cross-shaped shadow was sighted.

He wasn't a loser, and he wanted that gold. Slocum looked back at Holly and wondered at her avarice. Should he bother dividing it with her if he could find the hoard?

He returned to the fire and squatted down. Holly reached out and touched his cold cheek and softly said, "I'm sorry, John. All this is making me crazy. Things are happening too fast for me to understand. I'm still confused over losing Jesse that suddenly."

"We're going to have to find the gold now," he said. "Or we'll have to wait until next fall."

"Why?" she asked. "I thought we might head on to the Pacific and then make our way up to Seattle. It's supposed to be a nice little town."

"The shadow that marks the cave is going to move with the sun. It's been a month or more since Keegan hid the gold. The shadow might have moved, but we can make a guess where to look. In another month, we're out of luck."

Holly stared into the night at the storm gathering so powerfully around them. "We might not see the sun again until spring."

"Even if we can't get the gold out until spring thaw, we've got to find it now so we can locate it again."

She put her arms around him and nested her head in the soft lining of his coat. He thought he felt her tears dampening his shirt, but it might have been errant snowflakes pelting down harder and harder. The wind had kicked up and threatened to drift any snow falling into piles higher than a man's head.

"We've got to hole up for the night," he told her. "We're exposed out here. There must be a cave somewhere that will cut off most of the wind."

"I want to get away from here," she said, looking into the now dancing snowfall toward Silas Abrams.

"There's a tiny cave I spotted on the way up here," he said. "We can get there, build a wall of rocks in front of the entrance, and start a good fire. There's still enough dry wood available to get us through the night in comfort."

"He's dead," she said, almost to herself. Slocum wasn't sure if she meant Abrams or Jesse Keegan.

Shoulders slumping, Holly Hammersmith led the way down the side of the mountain to the cave Slocum had seen. She urged the horses into the back of the stony pocket and began fixing them what little grass she could find. Slocum brought back armload after armload of wood.

Each trip took longer than the last as the storm mounted in intensity. He was hardly able to walk upright against the wind when he dropped the last load on the cave floor.

"There," he said. "That ought to hold us."

"For days," Holly observed. Her blue eyes widened slightly. "Is the storm *that* bad?"

"It might be," he said. "Help me get a low wall of rock built across the mouth of the cave."

They worked for almost an hour piling up stones until they were waist-high. Only then did Slocum allow her to rest. Outside, just beyond the dancing curtain of their fire, swirled snowflakes that had turned into frosty bullets sniping at his exposed flesh. The sleet would form a nasty covering over the other snowfall and make traveling hazardous for days.

Slocum checked his watch. It ought to be a few minutes before dawn, but no hint of sunlight entered their small cave. If anything, the storm's fury had doubled. The sky might not show during the rest of the day.

Even with the shield formed by the cave and their crude rock wall, the wind crept in and stuck icy fingers into Slocum's body. He built up the fire, vowing to keep it going enough to keep warm but not high enough to use up their small supply of fuel. He knew storms like this might rage for days.

"The horses are all right," Holly said, seeing his concern. "So am I. I'm sorry for anything I might have done to hurt you, John."

"What are you talking about?" He dropped down to the cave floor and spread his blanket near the fire.

"I must sound like a grasping bitch. It's just that I never had anything until Jesse came along. With him gone, I lost sight of everything except the gold."

"We'll find it," he assured her.

"Right now, I don't care. Gold can't keep you warm on a night like this." Her fingers crept inside his longjohns once more and brushed across his hairy chest. Slocum started to say something, but the words were smothered by her lips. She kissed him passionately. Slocum responded quickly.

Warmth pumped into his loins, and his heart raced as Holly stroked over his crotch. He fumbled to get her shirt open and find the twin mounds of breasts hidden there. When he did she let out a tiny yelp of joy and seemed to melt in his arms.

"Go on, John," she urged. "Do it all to me. I . . . I want you so bad." She kissed him with even more fervor, taking his breath away. He forgot about the cold wind blowing into the cave and the smoke that caught just inside to choke him. The hard rock under him was forgotten, too, as she half rolled atop him.

Naked breasts pressing into his chest, Holly kissed his lips and cheeks and neck and ears. He pushed her away slightly and fastened his mouth on her goose-fleshed breasts. He found the taut, hard buttons of her nipples and worked them around and around with his eager tongue. He looked up past those wondrous snowy, warm mounds of flesh and saw her expression.

Rapture etched every line of her face. The dancing flames cast a pale orange light that made her seem all the more desirable to him. The heat mounted in his loins.

"I want you, too," he said. Slocum had been with many women over the years, but none excited him like this one. He felt like a young buck getting laid for the very first time. Everything Holly did thrilled him. Her lightest touch sent surges of pleasure through his body. And her lips!

He almost exploded when she opened his trousers and lightly kissed the throbbing tip of his erection. Her hot breath gusted through the tangle of hair around it, and her tongue roughly laved until his hips lifted off the rocky floor.

"I'm ready for you, too," she said, repositioning herself and nibbling at his ear.

Slocum rolled over and pinned the woman to the ground. Her legs parted willing—wantonly!—for him. His jerking tip touched her nethermost flesh and found warmth and moisture there. He levered himself forward slightly until the purpled tip of his manhood vanished into her. Then his control began to fade.

She was tight and hot and demanding around him. Holly pulled him down to kiss him even more fervently than before. Slocum's hips began to work on their own, sliding forward until man and woman were securely joined.

"You fill me up so much, John. I love it. I love it!"

She gasped when he pulled back from her clutching interior, teasing and tormenting. But Slocum's stamina was wearing thin. He had ridden hard, had almost lost his life a dozen times, had killed, had seen death. The cold sapped his strength, as did the high altitude in the Lost Mountain Range.

And, whether he admitted it or not, Holly Hammersmith was entrancingly lovely. The sight of her below him, wanting him, urging him on, sucked away his control. He began moving faster and faster. Friction mounted along his fleshy shaft. The woman gasped and moaned and began thrashing around. Slocum's hips swung back and forth in a regular rhythm that quickly turned ragged with desire.

He exploded like a stick of dynamite. She clutched him fiercely, pulling him close as he spilled his seed into her yearning center.

Holly arched her back and began grinding her hips in

small, erotic circles. Seconds later, she let out a long low moan that rivaled the wind outside.

They collapsed onto their blankets beside the tiny fire, lightly touching each other and exploring without words.

Holly fell asleep soon. Slocum continued to stare out into the dancing white curtain pulled across the day's warming sun and wondered when they would be able to leave the cave.

He hoped it wasn't going to be *too* soon.

17

Slocum awoke hours later with Holly pressed tightly against him. He moved slightly and she murmured in her sleep, turning and taking the blanket with her. He let her sleep. He shivered as a stiff, cold wind blew into the tiny cave. Buttoning his shirt and finding his lined sheepskin coat, he stood and finished dressing. The fire had died to little more than embers. He took a few minutes to get it going again, then went to see how the horses were faring. They stood restlessly at the back of the cave, large brown eyes glaring at him in silent accusation. He saw that they needed more feed. Getting it might prove to be a big problem.

He warmed his cold-numbed hands for a few minutes over the dancing flames, then went to the mouth of the cave. The snow was drifted level with the waist-high stone wall they had built. The worst of the storm had passed. Only occasional wet flakes fluttered down from a leaden sky now. As far as Slocum could see stretched an unbroken white blanket of cold, wet snow.

Shivering again, he pulled his coat more tightly around him and started out into the snow. The horses needed food and couldn't get it for themselves. Without the horses, he

knew they'd have little chance of making it out of the Lost
Mountain Range or Idaho Territory.

He spent more than an hour digging in the snow. It had
been a moderate snowstorm for an Idaho locked in winter,
but a big one for this late in the fall. Over two feet had
fallen during the night and the morning. It was almost
noon. He wished they could get out of the cave and on
their way. The longer they stayed in one place, the better
the chance they would be found.

Sheriff, cavalry, Indians—it didn't matter who found
them. The result would be identical.

He returned to the cave to find a meal cooking on the
small fire. Holly looked up, her face aglow.

"I thought you might like some hot food," she said.
"The fire isn't causing too much smoke, is it?"

"I could smell it but not see it." Slocum fed the horses
their sparse meal and settled down for his own. Everything
had come out of cans, but it might have been the best meal
offered in San Francisco's Pacific-Union Club for all he
cared.

They finished their meal in silence. Slocum took the
time to consider what they should do.

"I want to look for the gold," Holly said before he could
speak. "It's all I have in the world, John. I may not find it,
but I'd damn myself if I didn't at least try."

"Everyone in these mountains is looking for us with
blood in their eye," he pointed out. "Getting that much
gold out will be well nigh impossible until spring, even if
we do find it." He didn't trouble her with the additional
information about the gold he had gleaned from Silas
Abrams' feverish ranting. Slocum wasn't quite sure why
he held back, but he did.

"The snow wiped out our tracks," Holly said. "We

might as well have vanished, as far as the cavalry is concerned."

"Pinkham isn't likely to give up on us. He might not have a posse at his back anymore, but he's still out there." Slocum stared at the cave opening and the blue patches of afternoon sky poking through. He had a sense about such things. Someone was still on his trail—and not far behind.

"We've done well this far."

"Done well?" Slocum made a rude noise. "We lost Jesse, Abrams froze to death, all we've got in the way of gold is an ounce or two at the most. What does it mean to you to do good?"

"*We're* alive," she said. "We can keep hunting. We can outsmart any cavalry officer or sheriff they send after us."

Slocum wanted to go into detail how unlikely it was they could stay ahead of both posse and cavalry detachment. He shook his head, the memory of their run-in too clear for him. And then there was Chief Joseph. He had blundered into a Nez Percé war party and had almost lost his scalp because of it. The brave had seen how Slocum had inadvertently helped. Otherwise, Slocum would have been as dead as Jesse Keegan and Silas Abrams.

"More gold than you can dream of, John," she said seductively. "All we need to do is find it and mark the location. We can come back for it in the spring."

"We'll need money," he said.

"We take what we can," she said in exasperation. "Really, John, I'm beginning to think you don't want to be rich. That's what the gold will do for us. It'll make us both filthy rich!"

"Rather be alive and broke," he said, still staring out across the snowy slopes of the mountains. The gray clouds broke apart and left behind blindingly azure sky.

"I'll look for it, then, and you can go your way."

"I'll help. But not today. Tomorrow, at dawn."

"There's still time . . ." Her words trailed off when she saw how Slocum wanted to spend the rest of the day. By the time they finished making love, dusk had settled like a familiar blanket around the cold, rocky shoulders of the Lost Mountain Range.

"This looks to be a good spot to camp," he said, studying the small stand of wind-gnarled trees.

"So early?" Holly looked up at the sun, squinting against the bright reflection of light from the white fields of snow. "We've got another couple hours we can travel. The Snake's not more than that from here."

"Take a deep whiff of the air," he ordered. She obeyed and looked annoyed. "There's cedar on the air. We're downwind from someone with a big fire. I want to see who it is."

"But that means they're between us and the river." Holly subsided, seeing what Slocum was driving at. "Very well, John. I'll put together a lean-to for us while you scout. Don't be too long."

"I won't," he promised. He picked a path through the snow that led ever upward until he came to the top of a jagged ridge. Dismounting, not wanting to silhouette himself against the bright sky, he walked along the rocky ridge. The ridge had been blown clean by the strong storm winds coming from the west. For the first time all day he was out of knee-deep snow.

He tied his horse to a tree where sparse grass was available for grazing. Then he went exploring. The scent of wood smoke had strengthened when he reached the ridge. Now it was overpowering. Whoever was sitting around that campfire was either damned close or had a small forest fire raging.

Slocum discovered the answer: both. Not fifty yards away the cavalry detachment had erected a base camp. Slanting wood walls rose to screen the horses from the constant wind yet give immediate access and some small grazing. The soldiers had done almost as well for themselves. Some had burrowed down a few inches into the still-unfrozen ground for protection. Others had strung sheets of canvas over poles to fashion rude tents.

What Slocum noticed before all this were the patrols. The officer in charge had not neglected posting sentries at the camp's perimeter. Sneaking into camp would be impossible, and getting down the mountainside past the camp would be damned hard.

Slocum considered getting his Winchester and trying to take a potshot at the lieutenant in charge. A squad of troopers without an officer tended to make big mistakes. He had learned this during the war when he had looked for glints of sunlight off Union officers' braid. A single shot could turn the tide of battle.

Slocum forgot that strategy. He didn't have the army of the Confederate States of America at his back now. These were seasoned troopers in the camp; he saw that from the way they set up their bivouac. Two sergeants kept the men alert, and the officer was no snotty-nosed kid promoted beyond his ability. Slocum squinted at the distant officer and knew a seasoned leader when he saw one.

He slipped back into the sparse stand of trees he'd used for cover and made his way to his horse. The gelding looked up, seemingly disgusted. The horse had hoped for another hour or two of cropping at the skimpy turf.

Slocum led the horse down the backside of the mountain before climbing into the saddle. He didn't want a soldier roaming around the mountain to spot him.

He had almost reached the spot where he had left Holly

when he reined in and listened hard. Patting the horse's neck kept it quiet while he strained. His nose worked like a chipmunk's, then he squinted against the brightness of the snow as he tried to penetrate the small grove where they'd set up camp.

Slocum didn't see or hear anything, but something had spooked him. He had learned to trust his instincts; they kept him alive. Dismounting, he left his horse some distance away. He made his way to a vantage point just above the small encampment and dropped to his belly.

At first he saw nothing wrong. The fire was blazing, the dry wood producing little smoke. Their bedrolls were spread out side by side. What they had left of their supplies was safely stored, hung from a tree limb against pillaging by a sleepless bear.

When Holly didn't appear after five minutes of careful spying, he grew restive. Something was wrong. Slocum began circling the camp. When he found a second horse tethered beside Holly's, he knew what had happened.

Sheriff Pinkham had stumbled on their camp and had Holly as his prisoner.

But where? Slocum hadn't seen movement or any other sign of them near the camp. He returned to his vantage point and thought hard about what he'd do if the circumstances were reversed.

Pinkham was down there waiting. Slocum felt it in his bones. Where? How?

A slow smile crossed his lips. He didn't know where Holly had been tied and gagged and left, but it was close by. As to the sheriff, he was down there in the camp playing a patient waiting game.

Slocum made another circuit of the camp, knowing every second he waited made Pinkham that much edgier. More careful this time, Slocum found the tracks the sheriff had covered over using a broom of pine branch. He followed the brushed-out segment of the snowy path until he found an overhang. Holly Hammersmith lay there securely tied and gagged, as he'd thought. Slocum started to go to her, then stopped.

She'd be out of the way here. He didn't want to argue with her over tactics. If he finished off the sheriff, he'd be able to free her. If Pinkham stopped him, the sheriff knew where she was. It might be for the best to end this dangerous hide-and-seek.

Slocum returned to the camp. His fire had burned down to embers. Already the sun dipped low over the distant mountain peak to the west. In another few minutes, the camp would surrender totally to dusk. Slocum drew his Colt Navy and aimed at his blanket.

His finger tightened until the six-shooter bucked in his hand. A bullet ripped through the blanket and kicked up a small fountain of dirt.

Slocum cursed. He had picked the wrong hiding place. Pinkham was better at concealment than he'd thought. Already the other blanket was wiggling and flapping. Slocum swung his pistol around and shot square into the wool blanket.

He was rewarded by a loud yelp of pain. He'd winged the hiding sheriff.

"Damn it, you're a dead man for this!" raged the wounded lawman. Slocum got off a second shot, also a hit. Pinkham fell face-down in the snow and wiggled hard to reach a fallen log.

Behind him he left a bloody trail. Slocum doubted either wound was too damaging to the cursing sheriff. He also doubted if Pinkham would be able to move very fast with two bullets in him.

"Give it up, Sheriff, and I'll let you go."

"I've got the woman. She's dead meat if you don't surrender."

"Your posse's gone back to town," said Slocum, moving through the gathering shadows to find a better spot for his next barrage. "You're alone, Pinkham."

"You know me?"

Slocum didn't reply. The sheriff wanted him to give away his position. Slocum steadied his pistol against a tree limb and waited for the small target to grow as the sheriff poked his head up. He pulled the trigger.

The man's hat sailed into the twilight. The head under it slumped back. Slocum wasn't sure if he'd killed the man —or if the sheriff had laid a trap for him.

Slocum continued to circle until he got behind the lawman. Only then did he advance, taking his time, doing a sneak worthy of any Indian. Slocum kept his Colt trained on Pinkham's back as he knelt, wary of the pistol in the law officer's limp hand. Even after he pulled the sixshooter away, Slocum was cautious. More than one man on the frontier carried a hideout gun. He usually carried one himself.

Rolling the sheriff over showed where the bullet had cut a deep gorge in his forehead. The bleeding had slowed, stanched by the snow. Ragged breathing showed the sheriff was alive, but barely.

Slocum left Pinkham and hurried to free Holly.

"John! I heard shots. I thought he had you!"

"I'm too smart for that." Slocum helped her get circulation back into her wrists, then added, "We've got to get the hell out of here, though. The cavalry's camp is right over the top of the rise. They'll have heard the shots and come to look into the cause. I don't want to be within ten miles of here when they arrive."

"Did you kill the sheriff?" she asked, out of breath from trying to keep up with him.

"He's behind that log. He was alive when I went to get you. But now?" Slocum shrugged.

He and Holly quickly packed and got their belongings loaded onto their horses. Slocum took the sheriff's mount, knowing the man wasn't going to need it.

They rode back down the mountain minutes before the cavalry patrol came to investigate. Slocum thanked Lady Luck for waiting until twilight to take out the sheriff. He doubted if the troopers would be too eager to come after them until morning.

That gave him a small margin, but not much.

18

"The horse soldiers aren't stopping, John," panted Holly Hammersmith. She bent down and pulled away a branch that had caught at her horse's bridle. The fragrant pine branch pulled free. When it did, her horse tried to bolt. She held it tightly, but the loud protests the horse made could be heard up and down the mountainside.

"They'll pull back for a few minutes to regroup," he said. "They'll find Sheriff Pinkham and want to get the story from him. Then they might come after us, but not before."

He knew he was blowing smoke. If the sergeant in command of the small squad had any sense, he'd send a man back to their bivouac with a message to pick up the fallen lawman. There wasn't a hell of a lot that could be done for him, either in the camp or by the troopers. If Pinkham recovered enough to tell what had happened, the soldiers would ride straight on and hardly slow down.

With their quarry this close, they wouldn't stop.

Slocum looked at the tracks they were leaving in the newly fallen snow and worried. A blind man could follow this trail.

"Holly," he said, "go on down the trail another hundred

yards, then cut directly up the slope for the ridge."

"Up? Toward the soldiers?"

"Not toward them. You'll end up a half mile to the east of their camp. I'm going to camouflage our trail."

She glanced at the dark hoofprints left in the white snow and shook her head. "How are you going to do it?" she asked. "Those are too deep to fill by hand."

"Just ride on. I'll catch up."

"And then what, John?"

"We're going to sneak past their bivouac. That's the last thing their officer will expect from us."

Her blue eyes widened in surprise. "That's the last thing *I* expected, too. Can we do it?"

"We'll try. If we make it, we're home free."

That wasn't true, and they both knew it. However much a boast it was, it gave them both new hope. Holly leaned over and gave him a quick kiss. Slocum knew it might be the last he'd ever get. What he had to do was foolhardy to the point of being dangerous. He didn't see any way around it, though.

Holly rode on down the trial, the sheriff's horse trotting alongside her. He waited until she had vanished into the black night before backtracking. He rode as close to their camp as he could, then dismounted and approached on foot in the knee-deep wet snow. He heard the horse soldiers talking loudly among themselves. Trying to make out the individual troopers' gossip about women and drinking and gambling wasn't of interest. He had to know if they were going to pursue him and Holly.

"Get your ass back to the lieutenant," he heard a gruff voice order. "Tell him that good-for-nothing sheriff got himself shot up and that his quarry is loose and nearby."

"You be waitin' for word back, Sarge?"

"Yeah, I reckon so. Now get moving. We don't have all night. It's gettin' cold out here."

Slocum heaved a sigh of relief. He had a half hour's grace to work a miracle. He quietly slipped away from the camp and found several fallen tree limbs still holding their pine needles. He lashed them together with a few stray limbs from bushes valiantly hanging on to their foliage. He tied the end of his lariat to his pommel and then rode slowly, trying not to make more of a trail as he retraced his way downslope.

He knew an experienced tracker could see the trick in the light of day. If the cavalry followed in the night, they might be fooled. He doubted it, but he had to try.

Slocum got to the point where Holly had started uphill across a rocky expanse. This helped. He dragged the brush behind him as he made his way up. Twice he got off his horse and carefully worked his way back to see how the trail-hiding went. He shook his head in disgust. The blind man that could have followed the trail before would never be fooled. Even a tenderfoot at tracking would see what was being done to hide the spoor.

He worked at scattering snow over the trail from tree limbs. The fresh fall was natural and would force a tracker to circle to be sure his quarry hadn't taken off at an angle. But the single-minded way Holly went directly upslope would limit the amount of confusion the cavalry might have at this trick.

Slocum joined Holly an hour later. She paced nervously as she waited for him. Her hand flashed toward the small-caliber pistol she kept under her coat. When she saw who it was, she relaxed.

"I'm sorry, John. I should never have let Pinkham sneak up on me like that. I'd gotten camp set up and then—"

He silenced her with a kiss. "Don't apologize. The man is determined. That makes up for a lot."

"Are the horse soldiers determined, too?"

"Not as much, though they'll send part of their detachment after us." He told her what he'd overheard.

"Their officer won't risk too many troopers," Slocum finished. "He knows the Nez Percé will chew up any small force they catch wandering around. He can't afford to lose even one patrol or the other soldiers will start to rebel."

"I don't know what else we can do," she said, skepticism in her words. "We *might* be able to sneak past their camp. What if they hear or see us?"

"We ride faster than the wind," he told her. "We don't have much choice. I just don't want to have a horse break a leg in the dark. Other than that, I don't see any problem."

Holly wasn't easily convinced, but the lure of Keegan's gold kept her going. Slocum knew they had only a few hours at most before the cavalry started breathing down their necks. He wanted to be far down the hill by the time the soldiers found the right trail.

Slocum made quick progress, using the stars as a guide to keep on course, until the clouds moved in and hid the nighttime Idaho sky. The sharp points of the stars vanished, and darkly boiling, turbulent storm clouds replaced them. For all the fury aloft in those clouds, no new snow fell.

"How far?" Holly whispered. "It feels as if we've been walking forever."

By the stars, they had been working their way down the mountainside for only two hours.

"We're past their camp. I don't want to ride just yet. The wind is blowing up from the canyon. Sound carries in this weather."

"I feel as if I'm blind. I don't much like it, John."

He touched her arm in what he hoped was a reassuring manner. She didn't pay any heed to him.

He found he needed her reassurance more than she did his. He was as jumpy as a long-tailed cat in a rocking-chair factory. The sergeant in charge of the squad that had found the sheriff wouldn't be fooled for long by the quick brush-work over the trail. The soldier might wait until he had better light to keep from losing the spoor, but Slocum doubted it. An old-timer like the sergeant would be confident of his own ability.

"John, look at the path we're on."

Slocum smiled broadly when he saw what Holly was pointing at. The cavalry had come up this path and had trampled the ground thoroughly. This was the break he had been looking for. Their horses' hoofprints could never be found in the morass of mud, ice, and ripped up grass.

"We can ride now," he said. The wind currents might carry the sound of the horses to the cavalry's bivouac, but the sounds would be small if they didn't hurry. On such a steep slope, anything more than a slow walk was fool-hardy.

Best of all, the hashed-up dirt would hide new tracks.

Slocum watched as Holly weaved and wobbled in the saddle, staying alert as she led the way down the path. He followed, vigilant for any sound of pursuit. After another hour of traveling, he began drifting off to sleep. The rocking motion of his sturdy gelding lulled him, and it had been a long time since he'd gotten a sound night's sleep. The time in the cave with Holly had been decidedly pleasant, but not necessarily restful.

Slocum came awake when the horse's gait changed abruptly and he almost fell from the saddle. He blinked and looked around, not sure what he saw for a few seconds.

"The Snake River," said Holly. "We've reached the

banks. Now where do we go? Up- or downstream?"

Slocum stretched and rubbed his eyes, then got his bearings. He knew more of what to look for than did Holly. He had no reason not to enlist her aid, but something deep down kept him from telling her all he knew. He scanned the swiftly flowing river and then looked up to the pale, dawn-lit canyon walls.

"That way," he said, pointing downstream. He saw an outcropping of bright red rocks. There might be dozens of such deposits along the river, but Jesse Keegan couldn't have been caught too far from here with the stolen gold.

"Why?" asked Holly. The sharpness of her tone told him she wasn't going to accept anything less than the truth.

"Abrams mentioned red rocks. That looks mighty red to me. Do you see anything like it in the other direction?"

Holly looked and shook her head. She rode alongside silently, but he saw that she wasn't satisfied with the answer. Again, he wondered why he hesitated to tell her what he had learned from Abrams. Slocum pushed it from his mind. His instincts were usually to be trusted, and he wasn't going to change now. They had kept him alive through the War and after.

Slocum craned his neck as he rode, looking for a rock formation that looked like an old woman's hooked nose. The red rocks were a signpost, but their destination wasn't yet in sight. He wished he had been able to talk to Keegan before the man had died. Slocum was sure he could have gotten better instructions from him than Abrams had. Being able to interrogate Silas Abrams would have been a help, too. As it was, they sought the gold with only the flimsiest of clues. He went around the bend in the raging river and slowed. The river sharply curved back on itself in an undeniable oxbow.

Slocum's heart almost stopped. The gold had to be near.

"Are we there, John?"

"I don't know. I'm trying to remember everything Abrams said." Slocum studied the red rock outcropping, then almost laughed. From below, they looked like a giant nose with two distended nostrils. Shrubs grew in the nostril holes and shadows completed the image of old witch's hooked nose.

Slocum turned in the saddle and tried to find where a tree might stand atop the high canyon wall to cast a shadow at noon on the opposite bank. Dozens of dark holes festooned the side of the canyon. Any of the caves might be where Keegan had hidden the stolen gold. Slocum saw no way to guess which was the proper hidey-hole. They had to wait until noon to see where the shadowy cross landed— after correcting for the months of seasonal sun shifting since Keegan had buried his golden treasure.

"John?"

"I think we—" Slocum froze when he realized Holly wasn't asking him if they had stumbled across the gold. She was warning him. He heard the thunder of hooves over the Snake River seconds after she did.

"Cavalry!" he cried.

He looked for a place to hide and didn't find it.

19

John Slocum turned downstream and waved to Holly to join him in a headlong ride for freedom. There was no way in hell they could match the firepower of a cavalry detachment. Even if the sergeant had sent half his squad back to their base camp, he had enough men with carbines to put Slocum away easily.

Holly rode alongside him, head bent low. The sheriff's captured horse strained to keep apace, even though it carried no weight. Slocum saw there was no hope of escaping. The cavalry had taken them completely by surprise. He wondered how they had sneaked up on them so easily.

His greed at the nearness of the gold had robbed him of his usual caution. That was the only explanation.

"There," he said indicating a small canyon. "Let's try to find a place to make a stand."

"We can't, John," the woman gasped out. Her long, raven-dark hair fluttered behind her like an unfettered garrison banner. "There are too many of them."

"You want to try for the canyon and let me decoy them away?"

"No!"

He nodded. He felt the same way. They were in this

together, and together they'd get out. Somehow.

His gelding starting to tire, Slocum slackened the pace and guided the horse between two tall pines. The snow had drifted here and made the going even harder. He had to rein back or his horse would have broken a leg in the deep snow.

"There. We can hole up there!" cried Holly.

The fall of rock was hardly more than a few oversized pebbles, but Slocum wasn't about to argue. The pounding of the cavalry's horses sounded like a death knell in his ears. He hit the ground running, stumbled, and kept going. By the time his horse had come to a complete halt, Slocum had the Winchester out and ready for action.

"Take care of the horses," he ordered Holly. "I'll stand them off."

"I want to help."

"Your pistol's not much good. Did the sheriff have a rifle?"

Holly drew a Henry revolving rifle from a saddle sheath.

"Don't fire unless you're sure you're going to hit something," Slocum said. "We don't have much ammunition." He watched as the troopers came to the canyon mouth. It had been too much to hope that they'd race by. The wily sergeant leading them hadn't missed the faint tracks in the muddy riverbank indicating that his prey had taken to ground.

Slocum sighted carefully and squeezed off a round. A trooper to the right of the sergeant gasped and fell from his horse. Slocum cursed. He had forgotten the strong wind blowing down the canyon. Correcting for windage, he fired again. He might have ruffled the sergeant's feathers, but he didn't injure him.

"They're getting behind cover. I want to shoot, John,

but I don't think I can hit anything at this range. What do you want me to do?"

"Wait until you're sure. That's the only way we're going to get out of this. Every shot has to count."

He settled down on his belly and watched the small canyon mouth for movement. The soldiers knew better than to come up the narrow gulch on horseback. They slipped into the undergrowth and worked up both walls. It wouldn't be too long before Slocum had his hands full trying to figure out where all the bullets were coming from.

Slocum looked above him, hoping to get to higher ground. He thanked his lucky stars he did. Looming at the top of a small bluff was a blue-suited soldier. Slocum rolled onto his back and fired twice. One slug took the trooper high in the leg. He clutched at his wound and dropped to his knees. Slocum fired a third time but missed.

"We've got a wounded man on the cliff above us," he told Holly. "Keep looking up. If he shows his ugly face over the rim, put a bullet in it."

He rolled onto his belly and got off two quick shots at infiltrating soldiers. As he reloaded his rifle, they worked even closer. He glanced at Holly, who fearfully stared up at the cliff. Slocum made a quick decision.

"Let the man be. Help me with the ones in front. There might be as many as eight of them left." Slocum began firing until his Winchester's hammer fell on an empty chamber. As he reloaded, Holly took up the slow, steady fire. Slocum doubted that she hit anything, but it slowed the soldiers' advance.

Just as he started to sight in on the sergeant, the man above him fired three times. A heavy lead slug ripped past Slocum's ear. Flesh tore, and a fountain of blood exploded from his temple. The pain wasn't great, but Slocum's vision blurred suddenly.

"John, are you all right?"

"Awright," he muttered. "Keep firing. Don't let 'em near." He heard the voice speaking and only slowly realized it was his own. The sniping soldier's bullet hadn't severely injured him, but it had scrambled his brains. He felt strangely divided, his body on one side and his thoughts on the other.

"How do you reload this thing?" demanded Holly. "I can't get the cylinder open."

"Open?" He shook his head and regretted it instantly. A wedge drove between his eyes and pulled a curtain of red across the world. Focusing on the agony driving like a freight train into his head, Slocum forced himself to sit up.

He took the Henry and broke it open for Holly. She quickly reloaded, using a ramrod housed on the underside of the rifle and shells taken from Sheriff Pinkham's saddlebags.

"They're almost on top of us," he said. "We can't fight them off. The trooper up in the rocks will get us, even if they don't." He pointed toward the shadowy line of troopers moving inexorably closer.

"What are we going to do?" Holly asked.

"Surrender," Slocum said. "You might be able to walk away from this if you're a fast enough talker."

"They'll hang us both," she said bitterly. "And I'll never see a speck of Jesse's gold! *My* gold, damn it!"

Slocum fired twice when a trooper dashed across a small cleared area. If there hadn't been knee-deep snow, the soldier might have made it. Slocum's slug took him high on the shoulder and spun him around. He fell heavily onto his back. He kicked feebly.

"Go tend him, Sergeant!" yelled Slocum.

Slocum pushed Holly's rifle away when she started to

shoot at the sergeant and another soldier coming to help their fallen companion.

"I could have got him, John. What're you doing?"

"Playing for time," he said. "Let them tend him. It'll occupy a couple of them for a few minutes with something other than blowing our heads off. Might make them more disposed toward us when they do overrun our position, too."

"John, they're behind us. Listen! It's their officer with the rest of the detachment."

The ground quaked under the power of scores of racing horses. For a horrible second, Slocum thought Holly was right. Then he realized that the lieutenant didn't command this many soldiers.

The wild whoops and flash of war paint and feathers told the true story. Chief Joseph was leading his Nez Percé warriors directly into the wilting fire laid down by the sergeant and his squad.

The Indians raced past, getting the soldiers caught between two groups. Peering out of the canyon toward the river, Slocum saw the Nez Percé chief sitting placidly on his powerful white stallion, a rifle in one hand and the horse's reins in the other. Chief Joseph lifted his rifle and fired once.

Hell broke loose in the small gulch.

Slocum pulled Holly down behind the rocks as fifty more Nez Percé rushed from up the canyon. They thundered by, firing as they came. The cavalry troopers might have stood a chance had they been mounted and able to retreat. The withering fire from accurate Nez Percé rifles cut them where they stood.

The trooper who had been in the rocks behind Slocum and Holly rose and tried to pick off Chief Joseph. He fired once. The great chief jerked at the passage of the bullet.

Other than this, he made no sign that he even noticed such a minor annoyance. A half-dozen braves fired simultaneously. The trooper slipped down the front of the cliff, half turning in midair before smashing into the rocks.

"What are we going to do, John? We can't parlay with the Indians any more than we could have with the cavalry."

"We try to get out of here," he said. "Staying isn't the way to keeping our scalps."

Holly clutched his sleeve. "Promise me you won't let them take me alive."

"The Nez Percé aren't as bad as other tribes," he told her, thinking about what the Comanche or the Ogalalla Sioux did to captured white women. Of the tribes he had a passing acquaintance with, the Nez Percé were about the most civilized.

He still didn't want her captured by Chief Joseph. The thought of what they might do froze him inside.

"I promise," he said. "Now let's see about getting the hell out of here."

They reached their horses and led them down a wall of the canyon. Holly jerked in surprise when she saw him heading for the river. She pointed up the canyon. He shook his head. The Nez Percé had come from there. They might have accidentally stumbled on Chief Joseph's hideout. If he was right, the Nez Percé band would slip back up the narrow canyon and pass Slocum and Holly without knowing it.

Slocum paused when he reached the mouth of the narrow gulch. Chief Joseph rode back and forth, as if listening. Something worried the Nez Percé war chief. He spoke with two others decked out in eagle feathers and war paint. Whatever they were discussing, Chief Joseph wasn't convinced he was doing the right thing. Slocum could tell by the set of the man's head and the way he swung restlessly from side to side on the white stallion.

Chief Joseph abruptly swung his huge horse back into the narrow canyon and trotted off. The others followed slowly, heads swiveling constantly.

"The chief thinks he's missed a victim or two—us," said Slocum. "The others aren't sure, but they're not going to pass up the chance at more round-eyes' scalps."

"Their camp must be up the canyon. You saved our skins, John. Thank you."

"We're not out of this yet." He waited ten minutes before getting to his feet. He pushed through the obscuring wall of brush they had taken refuge behind and cautiously ventured out. He motioned Holly to remain where she was.

His prudence was immediately rewarded. Two braves stirred in the brush across the gulch. Slocum slipped quietly to his knees, then fell forward into the snow, letting it pile around him and provide a modicum of protection.

The braves argued until the one painted with bear clan symbols won. He motioned angrily. The other followed. A minute later, Slocum heard horses trotting away, going up into the canyon to rejoin the rest in the war party.

Only then did he venture out and scout the area more carefully. He found two other spots where the Nez Percé had lain in wait, wanting to smoke out any cavalry soldiers playing possum. He had outwaited them and could now continue down the river in search of the gold.

He returned to find Holly already on horseback.

"I got tired of waiting, John. Let's go find the gold and move on. This place is getting increasingly dangerous."

He smiled wryly at that observation. "I agree. But we won't have to go too far. I know where the cave is."

The red rock outcropping was prominently outlined against the sky from the mouth of the gulch. Seldom had he seen a rock formation that looked more like a hooked nose.

And the sun had risen up well over the canyon's rim to cast a shadowy cross on the side of the cliff. It fell directly on a cave mouth.

The stolen gold was within their grasp.

20

"Is it time yet?" Holly Hammersmith asked anxiously. "I can't wait much longer, John. I'm so nervous!"

The nearness to a fortune in stolen gold dust and ingots made Slocum feel the same way, but he kept it hidden better than the woman did. He stood under the hooked nose of solid stone and stared up. There wasn't any question in his mind that they had found the right place. All they had to worry about was the sun coming out again to form the cross on the caves.

When they had ridden up two hours earlier, just at noon, there had been a distinct shadow-cross on the side of the canyon. Clouds had come in quickly. The cross vanished, as if it had never existed. Slocum had tried to figure out which of the caves the cross would hit, but he couldn't see what had formed the shadow.

Atop the far canyon rim were several trees that might have done it, but he wasn't sure. The shadow had been more substantial than that cast by a tree. Then it no longer mattered because a light snow had started falling.

They had waited anxiously for two hours, Slocum trying to figure the difference in angle of the sun while they bided their time. About fifteen feet to the west was his guess where the true cave lay. But he needed to see the shadow once more to get his bearings. And the longer they waited in the canyon, the more likely they were to run afoul of Chief Joseph and his braves.

"John?"

"I hear it. Hoofbeats coming from down the canyon."

"Another band of the Nez Percé?"

He shrugged. It might be a roving war party returning to their hidden camp. He doubted it, though. The braves he had seen with Chief Joseph were too numerous. The pounding now echoing up the canyon had to be caused by at least twenty men.

"Cavalry?" Holly pressed, trying to get an answer out of him. Slocum kept his eyes fixed on the heights, waiting for a moment of sunlight to give the proper shadow.

The horses came closer, forcing him into action. "Let's get up there," he said. "Try to keep hidden from below. If it is the cavalry, they'll come after us in nothing flat."

He and Holly led their horses through a tumble of rock toward the base of the canyon wall. From this vantage point he had a hard time seeing the caves above them. He didn't want to linger another day waiting for the sun. If the storms started moving in from Canada, they might be here for weeks. Better to get an idea where the shadow might fall and start a search without the convenient guide.

"It was the cavalry detachment," whispered Holly, as if the soldiers might hear her over the thunder of their horses' hooves. "They're riding straight up the canyon. Chief Joseph will cut them to bloody ribbons."

Slocum hesitated to call out and warn the troopers. He had no loyalty to the horse soldiers, but the Nez Percé chief wouldn't show any mercy. If any were captured, they might linger for days.

Slocum shrugged this off, too. He had put up with too

much since leaving Salt Lake City to pretend to care about others who had brought him such misery. Sheriff Pinkham was probably alive—somewhere. The cavalry lieutenant had made life hell by helping the lawman. The only difference between the officer and the sheriff lay in the immediacy of punishment.

Pinkham and his posse would have strung him up if they'd caught him. Slocum knew the cavalry was more likely to have returned him to the Territorial Prison—then they'd've hanged him.

"John?"

"The sun," he said. "The sun's coming out again. Look sharp. We've got to backtrack along the sun's path to guess where the noontime shadow would be."

The lure of the stolen gold took Holly's mind away from the battle that was about to occur just a short distance up the Snake River canyon. The sun blinked once, a lead-gray cloud acting like a giant eyelid. Slocum impatiently moved to get a better look at the cliff face.

Shots rang out up the canyon. At first there were only a few. The sporadic gunfire turned into a full-scale battle. The echoes became deafening, and the sounds of horses and men in pain made the hackles on his neck bristle.

"There, John, there!" cried Holly. "The cross!"

He glanced back across the wide canyon and found the rock formation that created the shadow. He had been right about the shadow being too dark to be caused by a tree. A stony cairn atop the other rim created this marker.

He spun back and sighted in on the cave. His quick eyes found a rocky path leading to the cave. He could understand why Jesse Keegan had chosen this spot. It gave him a hiding place from the posse chasing him—and it made a good hiding place for the gold.

"Let's get up there," said Slocum. "The cavalry isn't

going to hold up much longer. Chief Joseph's braves are going to have fresh scalps tonight. I don't want to add ours to the string."

He and Holly made their way up the easy path to the cave. He couldn't believe this was it.

"Let me look, John. I'll look!" The woman bolted past and dived into the cave. Slocum studied the cave floor and knew this wasn't the place. He had misjudged the movement of the sun over the past months since Keegan buried the gold. He left their horses and worked his way farther along the rocky path. He found small scratch marks showing where someone had passed this way. He couldn't tell from the weathering if it had been a month or a year ago.

Slocum turned and looked back down the canyon. The oxbow turn in the river prevented him from getting a good view of the battle. The gunfire had died down. Only a few intermittent shots sounded. The Nez Percé had wiped out the lieutenant and his detachment. Slocum shuddered as he mentally pictured what had happened.

The lieutenant had become worried about his sergeant. The old-timer knew his way around, and the lieutenant wasn't any young pup with his first command. He'd worry and then send out a scout. The scout would come back with the information that the sergeant had ridden down the banks of the river. The lieutenant would have struck his camp and followed with his full detachment, believing the worst had befallen his sergeant.

And it had.

Now he fell into the same trap. Chief Joseph had much to rejoice over this night. If he wanted to make his way to Canada, he could do so now without fear of being hounded by the cavalry. He had just wiped out his only obstacle to escape.

Slocum turned from the canyon and examined the cave

floor. This looked more promising. Protected from wind and snow, the dust on the floor still showed footprints. Recent ones.

He began nosing around and found several rocks that had been moved. There was only one reason anyone would bother rolling such large boulders around like that. He found evidence of a small campfire behind one. Jesse Keegan had positioned the rock to shield the fire from prying eyes. Any smoke that rose would gather in the cave. The roof had blackened under the fire.

Slocum heard a noise behind him and spun, his hand reaching under his heavy coat for his six-shooter.

Holly Hammersmith stood in the cave mouth.

"There wasn't anything in that cave. Is this the one, John?" she asked.

"Might be," he said. He tried to figure out his curious reluctance to admit anything to her. He couldn't. They were a team, partners, working together to find Keegan's hidden treasure trove. He had no reason to be so close-mouthed. But he was.

Slocum wondered why but didn't have the time to work it out in his head.

"This must be it. It's got to be. Jesse would have holed up here for a day or two, so he had plenty of time to bury the gold. He had it in a single large canvas bag. That's the way we stashed it after the robbery. He carried it all on his horse when we split up."

"Why didn't you divvy it up then?" asked Slocum.

"He was afraid I'd be caught," Holly said almost shyly. "And even then, I don't think he trusted Abrams."

"I'm surprised Abrams trusted him with the entire take from the robbery."

"We were close to getting caught," she said. "Jesse knew what he was doing. He was going to be slowed down by the gold. Abrams agreed that speed was more likely to get us away."

"So Keegan got nabbed and you and Abrams slipped away." It made sense to him. Keegan was sentenced and put away in the Territorial Prison without revealing the identities of his cohorts. This was something Slocum could appreciate.

"Here," she said eagerly. "Look at the floor. It's dirt. This must be why Jesse chose this cave. The other one had a hard rock floor. It would have taken dynamite to dig in it." She dropped to hands and knees and began pawing at the dirt. Slocum watched for a minute, then joined her. The earth did seem looser than he'd've expected. If Keegan had a day or two inside to hide the gold, he would have had plenty of time to dig up the dirt.

Fifteen minutes of digging passed before Holly let out a whoop of joy.

"Look. Here it is, John. The edge of the canvas bag!"

Slocum rubbed his cold fingers. Even though the weather had lightened, the air was still wintry. The only warmth he had generated was from the action of digging up the hidden bag with the gold in it. Now his heart pumped faster and he saw that he was rich. The canvas pouch must have held twenty pounds of gold.

He quickly changed his mind about the weight when he struggled to lift it. The weight must be closer to thirty pounds. Thirty pounds of gold!

"We did it, John. We did it!" chirped Holly.

Slocum was not sure what warned him. A small movement, a shadow, he couldn't say. His hand flew to his Colt Navy and drew it—too late.

He turned toward the mouth of the cave and saw three Nez Percé braves standing there, rifles aimed at him. Just behind them Chief Joseph watched impassively.

Slocum saw he had no chance to shoot down three braves and hope to escape. He placed the six-shooter gently on the ground where he might be able to get to it if it looked as if they were going to lose their scalps.

"No," cried Holly. "I won't give it up!"

"Silence," Chief Joseph ordered. He pushed past his trio of warriors and stood in the cave, head slightly bowed to keep his war feathers from brushing the roof of the cave.

"We might be able to deal, Chief," said Slocum.

"How? You have nothing to deal with," Chief Joseph said. His eyes sparkled at the sight of the canvas bag. Holly had opened the top flap to reveal smaller pouches of gold dust. He reached down and took a leather bag. He hefted it. "You have nothing to barter."

"It's ours," protested Holly.

Slocum shot to his feet when Chief Joseph struck her.

"Keep your squaw quiet. I have no time to deal with women." Chief Joseph motioned. Two of the braves entered the cave and dragged the gold to the cave mouth. There one hoisted it to his back and walked off down the rocky path.

"What are you going to do now?" asked Slocum. "You have our gold." He judged the distance to his pistol and the likelihood that he could kill the Nez Percé war leader before the other two braves filled him with holes.

It didn't look good, but he'd do it if they were going to die anyway.

"Kill them," Chief Joseph said.

21

Slocum tensed to dive for his pistol when someone outside the cave protested loudly. Slocum didn't speak the Nez Percé language, but he knew from the tone used that the challenge flew directly at the chief's order.

Chief Joseph spun and argued with the brave outside for several minutes. He returned, his face as stormy as any cloud Slocum had seen since coming to Idaho. Slocum still estimated distances and his chances. He wasn't sure what to make of Chief Joseph's demeanor. The Nez Percé leader sneered slightly.

"You have a powerful ally. My brother speaks for you. He has gone so far as to demand a war council if I do not grant him his wish. He says you saved him from the horse soldiers."

Slocum looked past Chief Joseph to the brave standing with his arms crossed. He was the one Slocum had inadvertently rescued from Sheriff Pinkham's posse.

"Tell him I hope his friend was buried with the honor due him." Slocum remembered the brave's second horse with the body draped over it.

"My brother's wife's cousin now roams the Happy Hunting Ground," said Chief Joseph.

Slocum stayed quiet. Chief Joseph eyed him again, then spun and stalked off, his feathers whistling against his buckskins as he left. The other braves waited until their war chief had gone, then backed out and rushed off in his wake. Remaining for a moment was Chief Joseph's brother. He stood stolidly, staring at Slocum, then nodded once and left also. Only then did Slocum let out the breath he hadn't known he was holding. His chest felt as if burning hot steel bands had been wrapped around it.

He picked up his six-shooter and stuck it into his holster.

Holly was beside herself with rage. "You're not just going to let those thieving heathens walk off with our gold? You can't! It's mine. Ours!"

"We're leaving with our scalps. I consider that to be a damned sight better than I'd hoped for just a few minutes ago. If I hadn't rescued the chief's brother from Sheriff Pinkham—by accident—we'd be dead now."

"I won't let them do this!" she raged. She fumbled for her pistol and tried to rush past Slocum. He scooped her up and held her feet off the floor until she stopped kicking.

"Are you cooled off enough for me to trust you?" he asked.

"Yes." The answer was sullen, but he believed her. Holly sat cross-legged on the cave floor for almost a minute without saying a word. Then she looked up at him, her eyes filled with tears. "We lost the gold, but I reckon it's better to have our lives."

He allowed as to how he'd rather be alive and poor than dead and filthy rich.

She heaved a deep sigh, then said, "I suppose this is it, John. We've reached the end of the road."

He started to deny it but found himself nodding in agreement.

"There's nothing to keep us together. We ought to get out of here and go our separate ways."

"The cavalry and the posse aren't going to bedevil us," he said. "From what I saw of the Nez Percé, they're likely to be going north into Canada."

"I'll head south. You can go west. Even if there's still someone hunting us, they'd be hard-pressed to nab us both if we split up like that."

"I doubt if Sheriff Pinkham's dead. Bloodied a mite, but not dead."

"He won't give up. We've got to go soon." She heaved herself to her feet and went outside. The cold wind whistled down the Snake River canyon and blew her long, dark hair across her expressionless face. Slocum joined her.

"You really want to take different trails?" he asked. She hugged him close and buried her face in his chest for a moment.

"Yes, John. It's for the best. The memory. You and Jesse. Me and Jesse. Everything. It *is* for the best."

The Nez Percé had left them their horses, even if they had stripped off most everything of value and had taken Sheriff Pinkham's horse. Slocum counted these insignificant losses as a small price to pay for staying alive.

He and Holly led their mounts to the riverbank and then rode slowly downstream, away from the Nez Percé encampment. When they came to a crossing canyon, furnishing a steady flow of water into the raging Snake, they stopped. Slocum pulled up his collar against the icy spray rising from the churning confluence. Rainbows formed in the water drops high in the air and turned the area into a small, if frigid, paradise. Under different circumstances,

Slocum would not have minded spending a day or two here watching the river and the rainbows dancing against the now azure sky.

"This is it, John. Maybe we'll meet again," Holly said. Tears rolled down her cheeks. "And don't try to talk me out of this. It has to be. I know it's the best for me."

"You're probably right," he said. He bent over and gave her a parting kiss. Then he looked along the river. "That'll go to the west eventually. Want me to take this route while you go up the crossing canyon?"

She nodded, as if not trusting her voice. Slocum touched the brim of his battered black Stetson and put the spurs to his horse's flanks. The gelding jumped and then trotted off. Slocum didn't bother looking back.

He rounded a bend in the river, the canyon walls hiding him from the spot where he'd parted from Holly Hammersmith. Slocum reined back and stopped. He took out his brother's watch and studied its face. He waited fifteen minutes before retracing his path.

Holly's tracks led into the canyon, up into the Lost Mountain Range and back toward Idaho City. They looked larger than normal, though, and this made Slocum smile. He had been right.

Walking his horse to keep from making too much noise, he found the path leading back to the cave where Jesse Keegan had hidden the gold from his robbery. Outside the small cave stood Holly's horse. Slocum tethered his to a small rock and then loosened his coat. He didn't think he'd have to use his Colt, but he had stayed alive trusting his instincts.

And he'd been right in not completely trusting Holly Hammersmith.

The woman knelt at the far back of the cave and dug

furiously. Slocum watched in silence until she let out a small whoop of glee. She furiously scattered dirt in all directions and tugged hard at a buried strongbox. From the trouble Holly had with it, Slocum guessed it was heavy— even heavier than the canvas bag had been.

"How much do you think's in it?" he asked softly.

"A hundred pounds if it's—" Blue eyes wide with surprise, she spun around. Her hand went for the small-caliber pistol stuck in her belt. She saw that Slocum had his Colt Navy in his hand, although it wasn't aimed in her direction.

"That much," Slocum said. "Fifty pounds each makes a tidy little sum, though not as much as a hundred pounds for just one of us."

She tensed but didn't put her worry into words.

"I'll help you get it out so we can divvy it up," he said.

Holly laughed and went to Slocum, giving him a big kiss. "I didn't think I could fool you."

"But you had to try. Sixteen hundred ounces of gold is a real temptation."

"Especially after all I've been through."

"You'll be content with half?"

She laughed again. "Of course I will. But maybe we don't have to ride different trails. We can both go to the coast. Seattle's a nice town, or so I've heard."

"And there are winter storms coming," Slocum went on smoothly. "We stand a better chance if we stick together."

"And," she said, smiling broadly, "I can help you spend your half if we're together."

Slocum looked at Holly Hammersmith and thought hard about her. She had tried to do him out of his fair share and had failed. Slocum didn't see any reason to think she would try again. Holly wasn't the kind to go back on her word—if she promised not to try to rob him of his share.

And she was a fine-looking woman. He couldn't think of anyone he'd rather have keeping his nights warm, helping him spend his gold, but he'd have to watch the lovely woman. It was a long way to the Pacific, and the temptation might come on her again.

It was a chance he was willing to take.

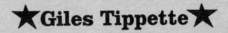